D1408141

Fate, Karma or Divine Intervention? (…take your pick)

Mark Whitney

Fate, Karma or Divine Intervention?
(...take your pick)

ISBN: 9798843758165

DEDICATION

To all who continue to battle addiction of any kind and to those who support them in their fight.

Fate, Karma or Divine Intervention? (...take your pick)

Fate, Karma or Divine Intervention? (...take your pick)

ACKNOWLEDGMENTS

This book would not be possible without the love and support of many. First and foremost amongst those is my wife, Joanne Brooks, who assisted in all aspects of this book and always encourages me.

A massive amount of thanks for their editorial assistance to my sister in-law Peggy Brooks, my step mother Linda Whitney, and dear friends Linda Buchanan, Alex McLean, Laurie Blaikie and Maureen Burgess.

I'm a fortunate man to have all of you in my corner.

Is this one better than my 1st? :) Hope you enjoy it.

xo

Mr. Whitney

Prologue

June 2005

"I don't get it. Why are you so anxious to visit there, especially with your dad now gone? Remember how they treated you in that town when your mother died?" It was a low blow, I knew it. But I just couldn't stand the thought of her driving all that way without me. And, truth be told, I was feeling pretty sorry for myself. The flu had brought out the worst in me. Needy, demanding; like a petulant child.

"Geoff, you know that's ancient history. Besides, I still have a couple of really good friends in that town, if you recall. Judy and Kate and their husbands all came to our wedding. Remember? They were my best friends growing up. Sure, it was a bit awkward for them at first with mom gone, but they came around. I've barely seen them since college, but we've always kept in touch. And now Judy has a baby girl, same age as Jenny. I think it will be really fun with the families getting together."

"You know what, Martha...? Fine, you go ahead. You want to drive four plus hours for a kiddies' play day, that's up to you. But I feel like crap. I'm not going anywhere. So, while you're enjoying a nice Memorial Day barbeque with your pals, I'll be having a great time self-medicating. Oh, and for real fun, maybe I can grade papers."

"Fine. Suit yourself. I'm going. Enjoy your pity party."

And, before I knew it, the car was pulling out of the driveway with Jenny strapped in her car seat waving 'bye, bye, daddy', and Martha giving me that look that said, 'I'm a big girl. I don't need your approval for this.' I never got the chance to apologize.

Part One

"Fate leads the willing and drags along the reluctant." - *Seneca*

St. Louis to Nashville, September 2007

As I rolled over, the newspaper that I had placed over my head in the wee hours of the morning, in a feeble attempt to shield me from the elements, or, given the balmy weather this time of year in St. Louis, to shield the world from me, shifted and exposed my bloodshot eyes to the bright morning – or was it afternoon? – sun. The irritation that the sunlight caused me was only surpassed by the irritation to my eardrums, caused by the passing ambulance that screeched past the opening of my hideaway. My head pulsed and throbbed in time with the alternating blue and red lights of the emergency vehicle, and within five painful seconds seemed to expand to twice its normal size. As I groaned loudly and tried in vain to cover my eyes and my ears, my stomach muscles contracted and the sound of my own retching was suddenly competing with the now receding siren. The taste of bile mixed liberally with that of stale pot smoke and cheap bourbon, giving my dry palate that all too familiar morning after taste. This was my final straw. In order to eliminate this taste I must somehow drag this living corpse I use as a body into an upright position and shuffle off to some source of liquid, preferably alcoholic, but not necessarily. My standards will never be accused of being high.

Thus establishing my immediate priority, I must now formulate a plan. The plan, as I see it, would move me from 'Point A' to 'Point B' wherein Point B is the spot where I may most likely find a beverage. My brain contorts at this thought and, during these very basic mental gymnastics, I come to the realization that I have no idea where 'Point A' is. Where am I? I wipe the crust from my eyes and take a closer look at my surroundings. I recognize the spot immediately as one of my favourite urban camping locations. I am wedged between two detached garages that, contrary to local by-laws, were built no more than three feet from each other. In fact, the overhangs from said garages practically touch. My bed consists of several eight foot lengths of old two by sixes (nails removed during one of my more productive periods) that rest on top of paper refuse. The head of the bed is as far away from the street as the chain link fence and bramble bushes that separate the garages from the backyards of the houses allow. I am, in fact, almost completely hidden from the world in this spot, which only receives relentless sunlight at around 2 p.m. Thus establishing my time and place, I feel a sense of accomplishment and, perhaps partially still drunk, make the bold decision to parlay this new found sense of purpose into an attempt to stand.

On the second attempt, I get upright and shuffle towards the opening of my hidey hole. I leave my blanket behind. I might be back, but even if I'm not, someone else will find this spot and use the blanket... while I pursue other blankets elsewhere. There is never a shortage of blankets to be found for the resourceful urban camper, and I prefer to travel lightly.

The heat is sweltering and I'm soon losing what is left of my body fluids to a small but persistent film of sweat that is slowing covering my entire body. While it is tempting to remove my jacket, and/or shirt and/or undershirt, I dare not. This would require the removal of my backpack as well and, it just seems like a Herculean effort for so small a gain. Besides, I now have a destination in mind that will soon eliminate thirst, allow me to wash my clothes, and offer some degree of temporary comfort against the humidity of St. Louis in September.

My 'Point A' is located near a small garage-lined alley that runs just off of Kennet Place. I shuffle down the alley to the road and head west. This part of St. Louis is lined with century homes and is well treed. Thank God for the shade, both as a means of shelter from the heat, and as camouflage. I refer to myself as an urban camper. Most would call me 'homeless'. However, post alcohol binges, I do still make an effort to clean myself up and have, for these past two years, managed to comfortably go about my business in this gentrified neighborhood without drawing too much attention to myself.

As I said, I travel lightly, with a small backpack that contains all of my worldly possessions. In addition to the clothes on my back these include: one spare pair of socks and underwear, one flannel shirt, one tee shirt (David Bowie swag circa 1982), one Swiss army knife, one pair of scissors, several plastic bags, matches, Visine, a Sucrettes lozenge container (which sometimes contains rolled joints and/or cigarettes), rolling papers, a map of the United States (complete with various city street maps) and a very worn copy of 'The Complete Works of Charles Dickens'.

I continue my slow progress west on Kennet, cross Mississippi Avenue and meander into Lafayette Park. The park is an oasis in the city, with dense foliage that blocks out sun and street noise. I have spent many days recuperating from my binges in this park and today, as I make my way towards the Grotto I can feel my body slowly respond to the park's soothing qualities. Perhaps in a few hours I will feel almost completely human again. But, before that, I now have three stops in mind.

My first stop will be the Lafayette Park pond, which is mere stumbling distance from the Grotto. I continue my westward shuffle on semi-auto pilot and find my usual entry point into the pond area. It is a quiet spot on the east side of the pond, completely surrounded by bushes. Thankfully, the pond area is deserted, so I can address my immediate concerns. I gingerly remove my backpack and strip down to my underwear. By this point, I'm exhausted and my entire body is crying for fluids. I wade into the pond and gently submerge my body under the surface. The weightless buoyancy, combined with the underwater quiet and the sense of my body acting as a sponge has me seriously contemplating just staying under until my lungs fill and I fall irretrievably into a deep dark sleep. But, my primal reptilian mind reasserts itself and I return to the surface to fill my lungs with air. And, like our first reptilian ancestors from time immemorial, I slowly drag my body towards the shore and the bushes where I left my belongings. Part one of my master plan is complete. Now that I have partially recovered from last night's debauchery, step two of my plan should be simple: to head over to the playground area that includes a public washroom complete with soap, running drinkable water, and paper towels. What more could a man ask for? I do ask for one more thing, actually. I ask that my friend and fellow camper Joey will be found at his usual bench, and that he will have something to drink. But, let's not get ahead of ourselves. After basking in the sun long enough to partially dry off, I dress and extract myself from the bushes. I feel somewhat better than I felt an hour ago, but, travelling the two hundred feet that separates me from the public washroom abutting the playground raises my heartbeat, which I can now hear and feel behind my ears. It physically feels like my head is expanding and contracting. To add to this misery as I get closer to the playground I cannot help but hear the wailing of a toddler, who I now spot standing by a bench beside a woman I assume is her mother. The woman seems indifferent, absorbed with whatever is happening on her mobile phone.

The child glances at me, and our eyes meet. Oddly, the wailing recedes and she smiles at me. She is a lovely little girl, who I estimate to be about two and a half years old. Curly brown hair, saucer brown eyes, and a toothy little grin that seems to span her entire face. I can't for the life of me see why my presence has so enchanted this creature, but, I smile back at her as I shuffle by on my way to the washroom. I see Joey on the other side of the playground and catch his eye, and we wave a greeting to each other.

I enter the washroom and make a beeline to the drinking fountain that is found on the west wall opposite the men's room. I drink greedily and the bile taste in my mouth slowly dissipates. I then make my way into the men's room, where I wet and soap two paper towels, grab a few extra towels and lay them aside. I then liberally apply soap to my still wet hair and gently message it into my scalp. This starts off as a somewhat painful process, but, after a while the throbbing in my head recedes somewhat. I find a clean cubicle, remove my clothes, and soap my body with the wet paper towels as best as I can. The last step of this morning's ritual is to rinse and dry. This is always the part I dread, because I have to leave the cubicle naked and quickly rinse at a sink that is convenient to a drain. Getting caught in a men's room in a public park naked is not a good look. I know I could rinse off back at the pond but even in my sad state I refuse to add soap suds to my soothing oasis.

I cautiously stick my head out the cubicle door, note the location of the target sink and drain, and, with the coast clear, quickly make my way over to the sink and splash water all over my head and body. Say what you will about St. Louis public works, but this park

14

washroom is always kept clean. I grab another few paper towels and return to my cubicle. I dry under my armpits, my chest and my genitalia, then take a seat and let the air do the rest. I get dressed, donning clean socks and underwear, and exit the stall. I'm reinvigorated and, as such, the third step of my plan now beckons. I must talk to Joey, and, with any luck, share in whatever he has. I need to intercept this early morning hangover/semi-drunk state and propel myself back to the full drunken stupor I so much prefer.

I shuffle out of the washroom and it is at that precise moment that I hear an ear curdling shriek coming from the direction of the pond. My instincts somehow take over. I find myself first walking fast, then sprinting towards the sound.

"My baby! Flora! Oh my God! My baby! Please help! Help!" The woman, whom I recognize from the playground bench, is now knee deep in the pond shrieking at the top of her lungs. My eyes quickly discern the cause of her distress. The little girl is in the middle of the pond, suspended face down and motionless.

Without hesitation, I yank off my backpack and hiking boots and plunge into the pond and, miraculously, finding my stroke from my high school swim meet days, I reach the little girl within seconds. I roll her over and quickly get her back to shore, while the young mother continues crying and sobbing. "Please save her! Please, dear God, save her!"

I place the little girl on the ground, tilt her head

15

back and start CPR. It seems like an hour, but probably only equates to no more than twenty seconds. On the third exhale from her lungs, there is a sputter and a cascade of pond water escapes from her mouth. Her eyes pop open, and the wailing, which only a short time ago caused my head to split, now sounds like music to my ears. I stand back as the mother scoops up her little girl and through her tears she manages to say, "Oh God! Oh God! Thank you! Thank you! My baby.... Thank God. You're fine, baby girl... You're fine. Mommy's here."

I stand awkwardly to the side. After a few minutes, the little girl appears to be returning to her pre-brush-with-death self. By this time, a small crowd has gathered, including my friend Joey with his bloodshot eyes and crumpled clothes. Somebody shouts, "I've called 911!"

The mother hugs me hard, and says loud enough for all to hear, "This wonderful man saved my baby girl from drowning." She turns to me and, her face full of emotion, says, "I can never thank you enough. I just can't believe it. You're like an angel. Flora, honey, thank the man who saved your life." The mother approaches me and the three of us have a group hug. Tears start to come, then stop, and I see that big beautiful smile again. My heart stops for a moment.

I'm now becoming acutely aware of the half dozen or so phones all pointed at the three of us, recording this tender moment. Our embrace ends, and the mother steps back and sets Flora down, keeping a firm grip on Flora's hand. She turns her attention to me. "You know, you are a hero... and I want to make sure you get the recognition you deserve. I just can't thank you enough! I'm Elmira Brown and this is my daughter Flora. What's your name, sir?"

Caught off guard, I respond with the first name that pops into my head, "Uh, Howe. Gordon Howe."

Elmira repeats this and asks, "So, tell me, Mr. Howe, do you live around here? I'd really like to do something nice for you... although I can't ever do enough to thank you."

"Uh, no, I don't live around here. Just passing through from Detroit really. And you don't owe me anything, Elmira. Really, just seeing that precious smile on Flora's face is thanks enough for me."

We briefly embrace again, and I hear approaching sirens and start putting on my boots and my backpack. Joey ambles over to me and with his toothless grin he mutters, "You look like you could use a drink, Professor, and by God, you've surely earned one. Come with me." 'Professor' is the nickname he and our fellow urban campers have come to call me.

"Joey, truer words have never been spoken. Let's go get drunk, my friend." With that, we surreptitiously leave the crowd and start to make our way towards Joey's bench. I glance back and see the rest of the gatherers still crowded around Elmira and Flora. Flora is watching me, and with her cute little smile she gives me a wave goodbye.

After a quick snort or two sitting on 'his' bench

17

in Lafayette Park, I'm feeling restless and want to move on. Joey insists we make our way towards the west downtown area. "We should celebrate with the lads. It's not every day you save a life."

Still in a state of shock and with the adrenaline fueling a restlessness I've not felt in a long while, I follow his lead and we head northwest. I know what Joey has in mind. The Gateway Park is adjacent to the Gateway Metro station. The area is teeming with homeless men and women, many of whom I've come to know. Joey clearly has a plan to parlay my Good Samaritan deed into a reason for our fellow urban campers to part with their various forms of intoxicating substances. Even though I'm still soaking wet, it's not altogether a bad idea, considering I still need to separate myself from the various thoughts clogging my conscious mind.

After twenty or so minutes of walking, we arrive at Gateway Park very hot and dishevelled. I say to Joey, "Let's go to the Metro station and splash our faces with some cool water. This heat is stifling and we might find some of the boys taking some time in the air conditioning." We walk through the park, across Chestnut Street and into the lobby of the station. Even though my clothes are still damp, it is a relief to feel the cool air. As predicted, we note a few of our acquaintances huddled in the northeast corner, squatting on benches laden with newspapers, discarded food containers and the accumulated debris of the previous night's debauchery. A few are staring blearily at the television hanging from the ceiling, which is currently streaming the twenty-four hour news station mingled with the metro schedule updates.

As we approach, Joey calls out to one of the TV watchers, "Hey Buzz, what's new, you old dog?" Buzz is a fellow alcohol appreciator who specializes in panhandling the station environment and has been doing that successfully for as long as anyone can remember. He turns his grey head towards us, and, as his eyes adjust to the light that is cascading in from behind us, I see his face shift from one of mild annoyance to a full out grin. This seems odd, since last I recall drinking with Buzz he threatened to cut my balls off when he deemed I had drank more than my share.

Buzz growls (he doesn't have any other type of intonation), "Well, if it isn't the man of the hour. Professor... you've done a great deed. Let me shake your hand and offer you a swig." I accept the paper bag Buzz has offered and, as I tilt back and savour the unmistakeable taste of Jim Beam, I glance at the television. The visual suddenly connects with Buzz's words and there I am, on television, being hugged by Elmira and Flora. The ticker below the visual reads "Local hero, mystery man Gordon Howe from Detroit saves girl from drowning." I take another swallow and hand the bottle bag back to Buzz. I'm speechless. Buzz carries on, "That was a good one... Gordie Howe from Detroit. But you did a good thing. You should be proud. You should think about a reward of some sort. I heard earlier that the lady was starting a fund raiser, to raise some money for you. You could be on Easy Street soon, Professor. Don't forget your good friend Buzz here, right?"

"Sure, Buzz, sure." I reply, as I take the bag from his hand again and draw another long swig.

Shit. I hate this... the unwanted attention, which I'm sure will soon include not just media, but also police. My head begins to swirl. My legs feel like they're weighed down with lead. I make my way to the nearest bench and collapse, bringing my hands to my head. I use the brief interlude, as others begin to realize the celebrity in their midst and offer their congratulations, to gather my wits and devise a plan of escape. Feigning sickness, I beg off from the crowd of my fellow campers, and make my way to the Greyhound ticket booth. The screen behind the attendant notes the next bus out is for Nashville, leaving in four minutes. I reach into my backpack and locate the envelope containing my emergency stash inside the liner of my jacket. "One way to Nashville, please," I announce as I hand the cashier a twenty dollar bill. She hands me my ticket, along with thirty-five cents change, and says, "Boarding now at gate five, just over there on your left." I thank her with a quick half smile, and quickly and quietly make my way to the platform, boarding the bus with just a minute to spare. I stumble to the back of the bus, finding the second to last row unoccupied.

As we pull out, I lean my head against the window, close my eyes and try desperately not to think of the past. But, I know this will be impossible, especially sober. It's going to be a very uncomfortable seven hour bus ride.

About three long hours into my Greyhound ordeal, the bus makes a pit stop along Interstate 64 in Evansville, Indiana. I consider making this town my next urban camping experience, but quickly reject the idea. The sun was starting to set, and I just couldn't face the prospect of trying to locate an acceptable place in this small town to spend the night. I've found that it's much easier in larger cities to find those seams in society that offer shelter and invisibility. Actually, becoming invisible is a skill set I've mastered, for the most part. As many of my homeless acquaintances can attest, if you try hard enough you can be invisible while being in plain sight.

The bus terminal includes a small convenience store that, mercifully, has a selection of beer, wine and liquor. My thirst calls for beer, but, in an effort to travel light, I select a mickey of Jack Daniel's. My stomach has been rumbling now for quite a while – I've not eaten a bite in almost 24 hours – so I decide to gamble on one of the rotisserie hot dogs. 'Gamble' is the word that most people would use, but, the reality is, for me, these hot dogs do not usually cause any intestinal issues. The secret to success with these dogs is to hope for a fresh bun and to apply all available condiments liberally. I am pleasantly surprised that this store offers buns that appear to be perhaps less than a day old, along with a plethora of fixings, including mustard, ketchup, relish, onions, tomatoes, grated cheese and sauerkraut. I've hit the motherlode. The foil wrap paper serves more as a container than as a wrapper as I heap mounds of sauerkraut, tomatoes and onions on top of the other condiments onto my dog, which is no longer visible. As I approach the cashier, who had been studiously ignoring me in a way that only cynical teenagers can do, he suddenly shows signs of life as he inspects my hot dog with mixed expressions of awe and repugnance. I dip into my emergency funds, now dangerously low, pay for my purchases and shuffle back to the bus, gorging myself on the dog as I go. As I reach the door, I stuff the last bite into my face, and hastily alight the stairs into the bus cabin. The mickey is concealed under my jacket and the driver nods to me, barely lifting his eyes from his cell phone as I pass.

I have four and a half more hours before we reach Nashville. The idea of returning to my restless ride and unpleasant memories motivate me to do the one thing I know will soothe my battered nerves. As I take my seat, I reach under my jacket and unscrew the cap. I slide the mickey of Jack Daniel's out from under my coat and in one graceful motion, begin to chug. In less than two minutes I've drained the bottle, which I wrap in a discarded magazine and deposit in the mesh sleeve attached to the back of the seat in front of me.

The hydraulic doors hiss shut. The bus driver mumbles something about 'the next stop' and the bus lurches forward. Within minutes the warm glow of an alcohol induced stupor begins to take my body on a separate, and infinitely more enjoyable, ride. I stare at the painted lines of the highway and lose myself, exactly as I intended.

I feel a shake on my shoulder and groggily open my eyes, blinking at the bright overhead bus lights. "Where am I?" are the first words I manage to string together.

"You're in Nashville, end of the line," the driver responds with barely concealed irritation. "Maybe if you weren't pissed to the gills, you'd know that."

I rub my eyes, gather my meagre belongings and gingerly make my way to the front exit. I hesitate, then say to the driver, "I'm not pissed to the gills, yet. But thanks for your concern," then raise my middle finger and alight to the sidewalk outside of the terminal.

"Go fuck yourself," he responds as he slams the door.

I enter the terminal and glance at the digital display showing the time and various bus schedules. It's nearing eleven at night. If I were back in St. Louis I'd only now be approaching my peak of intoxication, however, given I've just arrived in a new city that I am wholly unfamiliar with, I will have to remain somewhat coherent, until I find a place where I can safely catch my breath and stash my possessions. The thought has also occurred to me that, given my dwindling supply of emergency funds, I must soon, once again, take the unpleasant plunge into the world of the working populace. My objectives set, I make a careful study of the map of the city and bus routes that hangs from the terminal wall.

My eyes skip over the map and, to my surprise and mild amusement, land on Lafayette Street. Coming from Lafayette Park in St. Louis to Lafayette Street in Nashville has a symmetry to it that I can't deny. I trace the route highlighted on the map that runs along Lafayette Street, and, noting the route number, look again to the schedule and clock. The bus I'm looking for is arriving in twenty minutes on platform three, southbound. I amble over to the small platform, and find it crowded. There are at least a dozen people of all ages and descriptions, but the two that catch my eye appear to be like me, urban campers. A male, about five foot ten, with a scruffy beard and well used backpack is accompanied by a woman of similar height and slender build, also sporting a worn backpack and holding a guitar case covered in decals. Both look to be in their mid-thirties. Their hygiene is adequate, but I can tell their clothes are in need of washing.

I approach them tentatively and ask, "Excuse me, but are you two familiar with this bus route?" They look at me sceptically, so I continue, "It's just that I'm fresh off a bus from St. Louis, and only have the Nashville city map in the terminal to go by. I'm looking for a place to crash for the night, that's all." At this they recognize a fellow drifter and relax somewhat.

"What's your name?" the male asks as he eyes me over.

"Folks call me Professor," I answer, slightly embarrassed by the moniker, but not thinking of an alternative.

"Well, Professor, I'm Travis and this is Jenny. You're in luck, because we are familiar with this bus route and can maybe help you out with a place to crash." In my travels, I've become a bit leery of people that I consider too friendly on first acquaintance. Travis picks up on my body language and chuckles. "Don't worry," he says, 'we're not looking to roll you. We can take the bus with you and show you the shelter we're staying at on Lafayette. It's the Nashville Rescue Mission. They should have a bed or a least a blanket and quiet hallway where you can sleep."

I ponder this option. I'm generally not comfortable in shelters. The people who run them are often too curious for my liking. They always want to know who you are and what circumstances led you to their door. I've not carried any identification for a couple of years, and that generally becomes the first issue they think they need to solve for me. They insist that to get help I must first re-enter society, which is something I steadfastly do not wish to do. That said, it was almost midnight in a new city, my alcohol buzz was disappearing, and I'd just spent over eight hours in transit. A roof over my head and the possibility of a real bed was too much to ignore.

"I appreciate your help, Travis and Jenny. That sounds like my best option." They smile at me in return, and inform me that tickets may be purchased on the bus, which should be along any minute now. We wait patiently for the bus without sharing another word. This is one thing I've come to appreciate about the unanchored people I hang with. They tend to know when to mind their own business. I alight from the bus when they do, and follow them to the mission, where we exchange quick 'good nights'. I'm offered a cot and a blanket, settle in and drift into an uneasy sleep with my backpack as a pillow.

I'm rudely awakened the next morning by a bullhorn of a voice less than two feet from my ear. "Who the fuck are you? And what the fuck are you doing with your shit spilling over into my personal space?" The man with the voice has a pockmarked red face, a bulbous nose, and breath that smells like death. His hair is matted and the one tooth that remains visible is stained yellow.

"I might ask you the same questions," I reply, as I rub the grime from my eyes.

This temporarily leaves my assailant silent, but he quickly regains his bravado and says in my face, "Just mind your manners, newbie, or you'll find yourself on my bad side... and that's not somewhere you wanna be."

I'm about to respond with some choice words when I'm interrupted by Travis who is approaching my cot, "Looks like you settled in okay last night, Professor. Jenny and I are about to go for some breakfast, if you're interested...."

I nod, give ugly man the evil eye, pick up my backpack and follow Travis and Jenny out the door of the large room which I now see is full of cots. I'm not accustomed to sleeping around so many people, who are talking and farting and making other unwelcome noises, and as a result I had a very restless night. I've already made up my mind that this was the first and last night I will spend at Nashville Rescue Mission. But that puts some added pressure on me. I am in need of means to replenish my paltry funds, which will in turn allow me to pursue my goal of total inebriation that day. As we wander down a hallway, I notice the clock on the wall, which, to my utter astonishment reads 7:43. I've not been awake this early in quite some time; certainly not while I stayed in St. Louis. "Are you and Jenny early risers by nature, or is this for my benefit?" I ask Travis.

"We like to get an early start. You have to catch the morning commuters, or you might find yourself out of luck," he responds.

"And what is it that you are catching them for?" I ask.

"Well, Professor, welcome to music city, where, on just about every corner you'll find people like Jenny and me, picking on a guitar and singing for their supper. It's not making us rich, but you never know whose ear you might catch. There are plenty of stories about folks going from being a street performer to the Grand Ole Opry, almost overnight." Travis smiles, and continues, "Let's grab some grub and we'll give you the panhandler's tour of downtown Nashville."

We turn right off the hallway and enter another room, immediately recognizable as a cafeteria. A line of shuffling people has formed alongside a food counter that runs about twenty feet, roughly half the length of the room. The line starts with trays and cutlery, followed by self-serve items like yogurt and pre-packaged fruit salad. The last section of the line includes a server who is doling out oatmeal into bowls

29

for those inclined, followed by another server who is pouring coffee into Styrofoam cups. I follow Travis and Jenny's lead, and take one of everything offered. I've learned that these types of carbs are never to be turned down. As we get to the end of the line, it's clear there is one more hurdle before I can add sugar and cream to my coffee. An older man, maybe fifty years of age, is at the end of the counter and has a clip board with a pen attached that he hands to each individual. Everyone must set their tray down and sign his list, before they can sit and eat.

As our little group approaches he makes small talk with Travis and Jenny, eyeing me somewhat suspiciously. Finally he says, "You're the new one... I heard we had a new guest last night. What's your name? Please sign here, and after eating, would you mind stopping by the office for a quick chat? I'd like to get to know you." I reluctantly mumble, "Professor", grab the pen and make an 'X', which he regards with some skepticism, but doesn't comment. Instead, he asks, "Do you have any identification, Professor?" I shake my head no, and he sighs as I pass by.

We make our way to an empty table and sit down. I ask my new friends, "Who is that guy?"

Between mouthfuls, Jenny responds. "That's Eugene. He's a public servant, working for Nashville's Drug Addiction program. He's harmless."

I ponder this and ask, "He asked me to drop by his office. What do you think he wants?"

Travis replies, "Mainly he wants to claim

another feather in his cap, statistically. When he has his little talk with you, he can legitimately claim that he has another homeless or substance abuser under his care. The more people he has registered, the more likely it is he can retain or increase his public funding. It's a bit of game, but I understand why he does it. This shelter costs money to run, obviously."

I digest this information as I try to digest the lukewarm oatmeal. As an urban camper, I try very hard to stay out of the system. Having just arrived in Nashville, I'm very much inclined to keep it that way. I don't want to move on again so soon. And, besides, I don't consider myself a 'substance abuser' as Travis put it, I'm more of an alcohol connoisseur.

I quickly finish my oatmeal and coffee and stash the yogurt and fruit cup in my backpack for future use. As I'm about to leave the table I say to Travis, "I'm going to head out now. What say I meet you on the street in about five minutes? I really don't want to discuss my personal situation with Eugene, but I'd still like that panhandler's tour you talked about"

Jenny and Travis nod knowingly, "Yeah, he can come on a bit strong, can't he." Travis says. "Sure, we'll meet you on the street. Just turn right when you go outside, and walk to the next corner."

With that, I give Travis and Jenny a nod, and make for the cafeteria door while Eugene is engaged in scribbling something on his clipboard as he inspects a new 'guest's' identification. The front door is just a few steps away, and, as I exit and alight the stairs, I notice

31

for the first time that my hands are shaking. Lack of alcohol and a brush with officialdom does that to me. I make my way the ninety or so feet to the street corner and wait patiently for Travis and Jenny, who arrive a few minutes later.

"We got the old stink eye from Eugene when we left and he'd noticed you'd already split... guilt by association I suppose... but I think he'll drop it. He's a bit of a fanatic when it comes to registering new people," Travis says as we meet at the corner.

"Yeah, sorry about that. Hope it doesn't cause any trouble for you," I respond.

"No worries." Jenny smiles, "Sometime it's amusing to see him agitated. Anyhow, we're going to take you over to the entertainment district. It's just a few blocks away."

We cross the street and start walking northeast on Peabody Street. Travis starts his impromptu tour spiel, "This is the hotel district. Jenny and I usually come back here and camp out in front of some of the busier hotels around noon when the tourists are stirring a bit more. The Omni, the Marriot. Whatever looks hopping. Unless there is a bus parked out front... that means they're loading up and will be heading out on a guided tour. Then they usually aren't much interested in listening to us... they're too preoccupied with getting a good seat on the bus." He says this last bit with a sardonic smile, and continues on, "If you just head up north here on Fourth Avenue you've got all the venues where the big acts play, and then you hit Broadway.

Fourth and Broadway is Mecca, and that's where Jenny and me are heading now. The Grand Ole Opry is a stone's throw from that corner, and if we get there early like we are today, we get tons of people walking by, throwing change and small bills into our guitar case. With any luck, like I said, we're done there by noon and we go back to the hotel area to get the lunch crowd."

I consider my options. "I'll likely hang back a bit from the crowd and listen to you guys for a bit, if that's all right with you."

"Sure, that's great," Travis replies, "but whatcha gonna do for the rest of the day?"

I reply a bit awkwardly, "Well... I'm going to find a place to camp out. And, uh, I'm also going to try to find a bit of work." I don't know why, but for some reason, whenever I discuss the possibility of 'work' with anyone, it make me feel uncomfortable. Maybe it's the years of hanging out with people living on the margins, many who have long ago given up on the concept of work. But, these two clearly don't fit that description. I'm impressed with them. They seem to have it figured out; they live simply, enjoy what they're doing and just go with the flow. They're energized, it seems, just to be able to play their music for the tourists.

We continue on our path and we reach 'Mecca'. Jenny smiles as she sees the tourists, "I like our odds today. And I feel like singing."

"All right, Professor, we're going to start soon. Just enjoy the vibe of the city... and if you're in the mood, come by again around noon. I might have an idea of where you can find some work."

I nod at him, and shake his hand. It's seldom a complete stranger like this offers assistance.

Jenny unpacks her guitar, and straps it across her chest. Travis picks up the case and places it strategically a few feet in front of them, leaving about four feet of sidewalk between them and a big planter box near the curb. Jenny picks a few chords and smiles at passersby. Then, as she eyes a family of four who appear curious, she strums the opening lines of a song that sounds familiar to me.

Travis smiles broadly and proclaims to anyone within ear shot, "Morning, folks! We're going to play a little ditty called 'God's Coloring Book', sung as a duet by our favorites, Charlie Pride and Dolly Parton." And with that intro, they start into the song:

> *Today as I was walking*
>
> *In the fields just down the way*
>
> *I sat down on a fallen log*
>
> *To pass the time away*
>
> *And as I looked around me*
>
> *The more that I did look*
>
> *The more I realized that I am viewing*
>
> *God's coloring book.*

It's a pretty song. Travis has a strong melodic voice, and Jenny is equal to him, with just a hint of country twang, not unlike Dolly herself. I can't say this is my taste in music – I'm more of a Violent Femmes kind of guy – but it's hard not to be a little spellbound by the story they tell through the song lyrics. The family that earlier looked curious are now camped out in front of the guitar case, enthralled. Some other pedestrians start to form a semi-circle, leaving just enough space for people to walk by. People on their way to work seldom seem interested in tossing spare change to street performers – I know I certainly didn't in my former life – but a few slow their pace and do so.

At the end of the song there is a small smattering of applause. Some toss money into the guitar case and wander off, others stay for the next song – sounds like another gospel tune based on the opening lyrics. I've heard enough, so I catch Travis's eye and give a small wave. He smiles and nods, as they continue to play. All in all, it looks like they will have a lucrative morning. I, on the other hand, am almost penniless and starting to get the morning shakes.

It's now a little after nine in the morning. I'm not used to being up at this ungodly time; and I'm certainly not accustomed to being this sober. But, since I don't have enough money to buy booze, and I don't have the patience or energy to panhandle, I decide on an alternative plan.

As we were walking north on Fourth Avenue I noticed a small park. In my tired and hungover state I decide to backtrack, hoping to find a park bench to sleep, or at least close my eyes for the seemingly long hours until noon. I've made up my mind to rendezvous with Travis and Jenny again, to see if Travis's potential lead on employment might pan out. After fifteen minutes of walking, I spot my destination. I cross the street and spy a bronze plaque displayed on a sign along the path leading into the park "The Walk of Fame Park and Nashville Music Garden". It's not a huge park by any means, but it does offer some privacy along the back wall of a structure that appears to provide parking under the 'Music Garden'. The hedge at the back corner looks like a perfect place to hide under to catch a few winks.

I shuffle off the main path, towards the hedgerow. The ground is relatively level, the grass is well manicured, and it's very quiet. I plop my backpack down and rest my back against the wall, with the hedge quite effectively hiding me from street view. Feeling out of sorts, I reach into my backpack and find my Sucrettes case and my matches. I select one of the four joints from the container and spark it up. As I inhale, I'm reminded again of how parched I am, but decide that cotton mouth is the lessor of two evils. The joint does its work, and I find after a few puffs that I'm feeling much more relaxed.

After what could be a half hour – who knows? – of pondering life in general and watching pedestrians on faraway Fourth Avenue, I'm suddenly made aware that I'm not alone. There is a rustling sound coming from the hedgerow. I'm thinking it's likely an animal of some sort, and return to the tranquility of the buzz that

36

is now gently washing over me like a spring rain, when again I'm roused from the direction of the hedgerow. Only this time, the sound is of someone clearing their throat, and, in a very meek voice asking, "Hey man, do you think you could share some of that weed?"

Crawling out from the undergrowth to my left, I spot a young guy, maybe in his early twenties. His clothes are streaked with sweat stains and dirt. Faded jeans, a yellow tee shirt with a faded Nike logo, flip flop sandals. His hair is long and the left side is comically plastered to his head, while the right side is standing out at about ninety degrees. All this I take in quickly, but what really captures my attention is the six pack of Budweiser he's carefully cradling above the ground with his right arm as he emerges from the undergrowth doing an awkward one-handed crab walk.

"I'll tell you what, partner, I'll happily share this joint and others if you'd be willing to part with some of that Bud," I answer, trying very hard not to drool.

"Sure man. Here you go." He tosses me a can. I hand him the joint with one hand as I pop the can with the other. What a sweet sound.

I quickly guzzle back half the beer, then, regaining my composure, slowly speak. "They call me Professor. I'm new to Nashville. Thanks for the brew, I needed it."

The young man coughs, then offers his hand. "Name's Jed. Nashville born and bred." He offers the joint back to me, but I decline. This makes him smile broadly as he says, "You and me are going to be fast friends, Professor." I find his laid back pot smoking attitude refreshingly relaxing after having to deal with the loud mouth back at the mission house, Eugene the registration fanatic, and the morning rush hour crowd.

I finish my beer and set the can aside, and Jed, without skipping a beat, offers me another. "Well, that is mighty neighborly, Jed. Pleased to make your acquaintance. Let me repay your kindness," I say, as I snap open my Sucrettes case and hand him another pre-rolled joint.

"Fast friend indeed," Jed says, as he chuckles lightly. "So, where you from, Professor? What's your story? You don't look like your typical homeless dude... but given what we are up to at this time of day, you don't exactly strike me as a pillar of society either – no offense intended."

I look at Jed, wondering why he's curious, but decide to be less guarded than usual. "No offense taken. I arrived last night from St. Louis. I don't think of myself as homeless, I think of myself as an urban camper. I live simply and travel from place to place as I see fit. What about you? You don't strike me as your typical homeless dude either, to use your phrase....and no offense intended."

Jed exhales slowly as says, "No, I'm not homeless. I still live with my folks. But, lately things have been a bit strained, so I thought I'd spend the night under the stars. They don't worry about me anymore. And that's just fine by me." This confirms my suspicion. Jed is slumming, possibly sleeping off a hangover. I'm sure his parents aren't worried. In fact, they might be relieved. Jed has that alley cat, 'come and go as I please' attitude about him. This is probably the cause of the strain in his relationship with his folks, as he put it. Jed continues, "I've got a part time job, working the Predators' games and other events at the Bridgestone Arena... usher folks to their seats, then clean up their garbage after they leave. It ain't gonna make me rich, but as long as I'm living with my folks, I can save for school. I'm going to Nashville State Community College starting this time next year. Hotel Management and Hospitality. Lots of jobs around here once you graduate. My folks sometimes call me a slacker, but I remind them of my plan and that usually shuts them up."

Jed finishes the joint I had started, tucks the other one I traded him for the Bud behind his left ear, then stands up and stretches. "Well, Professor, thanks for the timely buzz. I've got to mosey on home and clean up. They got a Cirque de Solei matinee at the arena, so I gotta get ready for that. Here's one for the road, man." Jed tosses me another beer. I surprise myself and catch it.

"Thanks, Jed. And good luck with your plan. Just remember, your folks are having a tough time seeing you as an adult. Happens to all of us. They'll come around." He smiles, flashes me a peace sign, and wanders towards Fourth Avenue.

I quickly finish my second beer and pop open the third. Thankfully, I now have a comfortable buzz going. I sit back and ponder the few scattered and wispy clouds drifting across the bright blue sky. I think back to when I was Jed's age, trying to figure out my plan. That transition from being a kid to being a man. My foster parents were nothing but supportive, but, even with their support, it was an uncomfortable time. My life as an independent adult really started in college as a freshman. But, I can't dwell on that. Not now, semi-sober.

I drift in and out of a catnap-like sleep for the next couple of hours, then figure it's time to hook up with Travis and Jenny again. As I approach their corner, I see the crowd has grown from a half dozen to two dozen. People are clapping and laughing, as I hear Jenny belting out a George Jones tune, 'Honky Tonk Song':

I saw those blue lights flashin'
Over my left shoulder
He walked right up and said,
"Get off that riding mower."
I said sir, "Let me explain
Before you put me in the tank."
She took my keys away
And now she won't drive me to drink.

I need a honky tonk song, a cold, cold beer
A hardwood floor, a smoky atmosphere
A pocket full of change to last me all night

long
I gotta hear old Hank a moanin' a honky tonk
song.

As she finishes up, people drop small bills and coins into the guitar case. Travis says to nobody in particular, "Thanks folks. If you want to catch another performance, we'll be playing the open mic tonight at Martin's Bar-B-Q Joint, just a stone's throw south on Fourth Avenue." Jenny collects the cash from the guitar case and hands it to Travis, who quickly pockets the coins and places the rest in a billfold he's pulled from his front pocket. Once the guitar is safely stashed, Jenny looks up and smiles at me.

"Well, what did you think?" she asks.

"Uh, the gospels aren't exactly my thing, but that last one I caught, I really liked. I can certainly identify," I answer.

She laughs lightly. Travis says, "So you heard about our gig tonight then, too. That's where we're heading now."

I look at him. Not sure he's as warm to me as he was earlier this morning. Then I realize why. Here's a guy who's offered to put his neck out for me to try to find some employment and I show up with red eyes and smelling of beer and pot. "Hey, Travis... sorry, man. I just needed a little something to help me get through the morning. I'll be okay, I promise."

He looks at me, pensively nods, then quietly

41

says something to Jenny. She reaches into her handbag and hands me a stick of Juicy Fruit gum. "We can use the john at the Dunkin' Donuts just around the corner to clean you up a bit."

I feel a bit sheepish, but agree with him. I need to clean up my act if I have any hope of re-entering the working world. "Thanks. I promise I won't embarrass you."

We head out, and, as promised, we stop at a Dunkin' Donut's washroom. I scrub my face, slick back my hair and rinse my mouth. I reach into my backpack and find the Visine I've been hanging on to. I've seldom felt the need to use it, but now's the time. My eyes clear up quickly as we continue the several blocks towards Martin's Bar-B-Q. We pass the park I had just left, and in a few more blocks, there it is.

The building is non-descript, yet makes an impression because it seems out of place amongst the gleaming hotels that surround it. It is brown and square, with large multi paned windows. The entire effect is that of a re-purposed industrial site. You would not know it was a restaurant except for the garish neon sign that hangs over the sidewalk advertising it as such. We enter through the front door, and it's a continuation of the industrial motif. The ceiling is visible through the ancient wood rafters. Plank tables are surrounded by steel stools. A large bar runs the length of the south wall, offering everything from local craft beers to Tennessee moonshine. The east wall is what catches the eye though, as it is not a wall at all, but rather a

42

series of garage doors, all open to a courtyard. The courtyard is dominated by two ten foot long stainless steel half-drums that are the barbeque rotisseries, surrounded by picnic tables. The air is filled with the mouth-watering smell of hickory smoke and barbeque sauce, and, even though my stomach often rejects food unless it's accompanied by alcohol it starts to grumble with hunger. On the far west side of the courtyard, a small stage with a few footlights and overhead hanging spotlights completes the scene, which reminds me more of a family reunion setting rather than of a restaurant. Casual, comfy and inviting.

Jenny interrupts my reverie. "Professor, I can hear your stomach growling. This place has that effect on people." She smiles.

Travis has left us in the courtyard and now returns with a large bearded black man, who looks to be at least six foot four and pushing three hundred pounds. He's wearing jeans and a white apron over a white tee shirt, stained liberally with barbeque sauce. Travis makes the introductions, "Professor, this here is Martin, the owner of this fine establishment."

I hold out my hand and, Martin, smiling broadly, smothers it with his huge hand and says, "Pleasure to meet you, Professor." His smile is infectious.

I smile back. "The pleasure is mine, Martin. And might I add, this place is really something."

"We like to think so," Martin responds with a wink. He then steps back and looks me up and down, like I could be a prize pig about to be next on the rotisserie. After a few awkward seconds, he turns to me and asks, "Have you ever worked in a kitchen, Professor?"

I'm taken aback by the suddenness of this impromptu interview and stumble over my answer, "Well, uh, yes, I have some experience, but nothing more than busboy, dishwasher and occasional fast fry cook."

He looks at Travis and says, "I believe we can offer the Professor some work." He grins at me and adds, "All right then, let's put you to work. Here's what I will do for you. Come back here at around two-thirty today. You do the pots and pans, should take you a couple of hours. Then come back again around nine-thirty tonight, and you'll do the same thing. After that, you clean the kitchen. Should take you to about one in the morning. For your work I'm willing to give you the cot in the back room, use of the staff washroom, one meal, and twenty bucks a day. You get Sunday off. That's it... take it or leave it. Oh, and if you miss a shift, you're done."

Slightly taken aback, I ponder the offer. I'd be working for less than $3.50 an hour. But, on the other hand, that food smelled good. The bar looked enticing, as did the thought of a safe place to crash. Best of all, the hours seemed to align nicely with my lifestyle, meaning I would have the time, the funds and the sleeping arrangements to allow me to drink into the wee hours of the morning.

"Okay. I'm in,"

Martin slaps me on the back. "All right then. Let's have some pulled pork and a beer to seal the deal."

One beer turns to three as Martin orders his staff around through the midday lunch crowd, between regaling me with stories of his past, the restaurant, and whatever else comes to his mind. He's a very talkative guy, but his banter is pleasant and keeps me wakeful while the beers maintain the buzz from my morning tokes and brews.

Before I know it, my first shift at Martin's begins. Martin glances at his watch mid-sentence, "Oh, Lord. Look at the time. We both have work to do. You see that door at the far end of the bar? That says 'Staff Only, Do Not Enter'?... well, you go on ahead and enter. You're staff now. Habib, my sous chef, he'll point you in the right direction. Then you can show yourself around." And with that, the big man, moving with the speed and agility of an NFL wide receiver on a button hook route, makes his way towards the rotisseries.

I down what's left of my beer, and start towards the Staff Only sign. I catch Travis and Jenny's eyes. They've been chatting with someone who's been lingering around the stage, probably discussing tonight's 'open mic' session. I give them a smile and slight wave; they return the gesture.

I walk through the Staff Only door and see that the depth of the building is more than I originally thought. A hallway runs about twenty feet ahead. I deduce as I'm nearing a Dutch door with the top half open, that it leads into the kitchen. I notice another door, about two thirds down the hall, marked 'Staff Washroom', and a third door at the end of the hallway – a mystery for now, but I assume it's a small office or broom closet.

I peer into the open Dutch door and see the back of a short swarthy man wearing sandals, cut-off jean shorts and an apron. I tap on the door and clear my throat, as a way of announcing my presence. The man whirls towards me with a startled and perplexed look. Before he can process the apparition before him, I speak, "Hello. You must be Habib. They call me Professor. Martin hired me to wash dishes and help out, said you'd point me in the right direction."

I'm pleased to see the look on Habib's face change to a grin. He beckons, "Yes, yes! Please, come in, come in. You are a blessing from Allah! I thought I'd never see help again. Come. Come. I will show you what to do!"

I walk into the kitchen and immediately see that Habib is indeed overwhelmed. He catches my eye and says, "Yes, I know, it is a mess. But it is all I can do to keep up with the food orders during the noon rush. Then after that, I must start immediately to prepare for the dinner crowd. All of the pork is prepared in here – the marinades, the rubs, that is all me. And I have to make the salads – potato salad, bean salad, and more salads. I talked Martin into expanding the menu to include hummus, pita bread, falafels. All I make fresh every day. He has no idea how much I do. He runs me

46

ragged. He knows not everyone eats pork. He should thank me for the vegetarian patrons I bring here."

Suddenly Habib catches himself. His torrent of words ends and he shrugs, "But, merciful Allah, you are here now. I show you. First, we go to the crash table. All the dirty dishes and cutlery are there. You clean off plates and load them there, in the dishwasher." I look to the left and see trays sitting on a conveyor. It's a big industrial size washer. Habib continues, "Usually you need two or three cycles to do all of the dishes. You put dried dishes back on these carts." He points to two carts currently lodged under the countertop where he was working. "While loads are running through the dishwasher, you can wash the pots and pans here." He points to a big double sink that is full of medium and large pots, as well as heating trays. "Then, with dishes done, you wipe down all the surfaces and mop the floor. Any questions?"

It's a flood of information, but after thinking for a moment, I only have one question, "Yes. Where are the cleaning supplies?"

Habib eyes me, somewhat suspiciously, as if he's never been asked this question before. Then he jerks his head and says, "Follow." He walks briskly across the kitchen to the Dutch door, and down the hall to the mystery door at the end. He jerks the door open and points. I peer inside. It's a narrow space, roughly six feet across and eight feet in length. Just inside the door, to my right is a steel framed shelving unit, where various cleaning solutions and other assorted items like light bulbs, plumbing supplies, and, oddly, an Elvis bobble head are perched. Under the lower shelf, a bucket with a wringer and mop. On the left, a small desk with a set of drawers appears to be the financial hub of the establishment. An ancient adding machine, with a coil of adding paper spilling onto the desk, is accompanied by a ledger book and a small lamp. A chair is shoved under the desk.

At the far end of room, running the entire width of the room, is an army cot. And, much to my surprise and pleasure, a door with a wire mesh window is directly next to the desk, just beside the foot of the cot. I see this will be my new cubby hole. I make my way into the room, and relieve myself of my backpack, depositing it on the cot.

Habib looks at me, again with a hint of suspicion, and again shrugs and says, "So, I guess Martin has taken you in like a stray. And you now know where everything. Well, blessed be to Allah, you are here. It is time to work. Come." He makes a hasty retreat and we are both at work in the kitchen before I know what's hit me.

He's a herky jerky guy, ceaselessly bantering with himself in what I assume is Arabic. When he does address me, it's usually followed by a shrug, as if accepting his fate and my place in this kingdom. He's not unpleasant, and as he sees me working diligently, I can tell he is as grateful as his frequent 'Thanks be to Allah' indicate. And, even in my semi-hungover, buzzed state, I can also understand why he is thankful. This kitchen will be more than enough work for two of us.

As my first shift at Martin's comes to an end with the emptying of the mop bucket and a return of the mop and bucket to the office/ broom closet/ bedroom, I eye the army cot in a semi daze, and the events of the day finally catch up to me. I drag myself across the room, lower myself onto the cot and before I realize it, I'm in a coma-like sleep.

Nashville to Atlanta, August 2009

As I slowly surface to consciousness, I surmise it must be approaching my usual afternoon shift start, as I can hear Habib smashing pots and pans around, grumbling in Arabic and basically trying to stir me from the army cot without actually coming into the room. This is his way of telling me that he knows I'm hungover and he does not approve. Sort of like the mother of a nineteen-year-old would act if she knew her kid had just indulged in a bender and was in need of a 'lesson'. Only, I'm not nineteen. I'm approaching my mid-thirties. And Habib isn't my mom. Right now he's an annoying co-worker who should know better than to do this to me.

After almost two years of a very predictable routine, you'd think he would have the courtesy to not be that guy. I reluctantly roll out of the cot and wander down the hall to the staff washroom. The usual routine – splash face with cold water, sponge bath, slick back hair, brush teeth vigorously, take two Tylenols – is followed by a slow death march to the kitchen, where Habib greets me the same way he has done every day, "Ah, he is alive and ready for work, Allah be praised. I do hope the noise from my work didn't disturb you, Professor."

The days have blended together like this, with little variance. Wake up and do the afternoon shift. Stumble out into the late afternoon sun to find a six pack of beer. Smoke the occasional joint with Jed, who has taken almost permanent residence by the back hedge at the Music Garden park. Sometimes share alcohol with other like-minded urban campers. (We are on an honour system. I've bought more often than not, and many owe me, but I don't take advantage of this fact. I often buy an additional six pack or a mickey to share.) Make my way back to Martin's for the night shift. Usually I get there a bit early to chit chat with Martin, who, unlike a certain employee, is not judgemental about my drinking habits. He's a very decent guy. Martin will usually take a quick break when I arrive and we'll have a couple of fingers of Jack Daniel's, neat. By this time, I'm feeling pretty good. I've become fairly proficient in my work and generally finish my nightly duties around midnight, then, if the band's still on and has talent, I'll return to the bar with my hip flask and proceed to get ripped. Often if Travis and Jenny are playing, they will linger behind after close and Martin will share a bit more Jack Daniel's. If they aren't playing at Martin's, sometimes I will seek them out at other establishments, but that is a rarity – usually I just head out with my backpack and drink on the street somewhere. Victory Park, a good forty minute walk from Martin's, is where I often end up. Many of my drinking companions enjoy the park or congregate under the bridge that crosses the Cumberland River just east of the park. I drink into the wee hours of the morning, sleep through the rush hour traffic on Highway 41, and rouse myself mid-morning. Then I stumble back to my army cot to try to sleep off most of the hangover before I start the daily routine again. On my day off, I spend a little more time on my personal hygiene – wash my hair and do a total body scrub, and find a coin laundry. True to his word, Martin has kept his end of the bargain. And, like the responsible adult I am, regardless of how hungover I am or how inebriated, I've yet to miss a shift. Overall, it's exactly the comfortably numb existence I prefer.

Until it happens again.

It's around eleven a.m. and I'm about halfway back to my cot after a night's drinking. It's brutally hot and humid, as Nashville gets sometimes. As I'm approaching Broadway from the north I see a commotion in a parking lot, the Rosa Parks lot to be precise. I think to myself in my haze how ludicrous it is to name a parking lot after a hero of the civil rights movement, but, as I get nearer, the clamour of the commotion intensifies. A large group of Asian tourists has gathered around a car, some shouting and waving their hands frantically. Others are actually pounding on the car's windows. One man is on the hood, thumping on the windshield. It's an odd and disturbing sight and before my brain registers what my feet have done, I find myself propelled right into the midst of it.

None of the tourists are younger than sixty, would be my guess. But all are equally persistent in their intense desire to batter the car. As I approach the car, I see in the driver's seat what initially appears to be the cause of their consternation. A young woman, mid-twenties in appearance, is leaned back in the driver's seat, her mouth wide open, eyes bulging and a string of

52

vomit running from her chin down her neck and on to her tee shirt. Her bare left arm has rubber tubing hanging loosely above her elbow. By her pallor, she unfortunately appears dead. On her lap the cause of death is obvious – a used syringe.

But, wait, there is something else. As the scene becomes clear and my mind finally catches up, I notice for the first time this woman is not alone in the car. On the back passenger side, there is a baby strapped into a car seat, a boy based on the blue outfit. He's moving lethargically, rolling his head from side to side, but what strikes me immediately is that this baby's face is beet red. I suddenly realize he is suffering from extreme heat, and that is why these tourists are all frantically trying to break the car's windows.

Without hesitating, I reach into my backpack and pull out my Swiss army knife. It's not much, but it's solid and a much better option than breaking a fist. I move to the driver's window and, aiming for the middle, swing the closed knife with a hard arcing motion. The window cracks. I bring back my arm and repeat the motion, and the window shatters. Reaching inside, I quickly disengage the car locks and shout that the doors are unlocked. The tourists have been watching me, and relief sweeps over their faces. An elderly woman on the passenger side, who had managed to keep her wits about her, quickly opens the rear door, unbuckles and takes the baby from the car seat. The child is not crying, which is very concerning. Another woman appears with some bottled water, which I grab. I pull my spare socks from my backpack, soak one in water and start to towel the baby's forehead, shouting for someone to call 911. By now, I've noticed many of the tourists have pulled out their cell phones and, unbelievably, are taking video footage. I'm irritated by this, but am too preoccupied at the moment to worry about it.

The baby is awake now and sucking moisture from my sock, and his colour is not as alarming as it was only minutes ago. Nonetheless, I sense he is still in major discomfort. At this point, another man, whom I would guess to be about forty-five, arrives on the scene. He is wearing a uniform of sorts, and I surmise he might be the tour bus driver. He's out of breath, doubled over, but he manages to croak out, "Damn cell phones. Useless. I found.... pay phone.... ambulance... coming..."

I appear to be the only one in the crowd that hears and understands him. Two women have taken charge of the baby; some tourists are now moving back onto the bus, and others have formed little discussion groups, seemingly comparing cell phone videos. One of them approaches me, takes my hand and through a broad smile says to me, "Hero." He holds his phone, which shows in vivid detail the violent smash of the car window caused by me and my Swiss army knife. I think that, ironically, the cell phones in this case were useless as phones, but worked well for pictures and videos.

I soon hear the ambulance approaching and, as the man lets go of my hand, the now partially recovered bus driver asks me, "Was it you who did that? Did you smash that car window and get that baby out of there?"

I stare at him, at a loss for words, then shake my head and start to move away.

"Hey, wait a minute, man. Come back. You're a hero! At least tell us your name." I turn to him and blurt out the first name that comes to mind, "I'm, uh, Brett Hull... just visiting from St. Louis." He looks at me with a hint of incredulity, and I turn and continue my retreat. As I'm putting more distance between me and the parking lot the ambulance pulls up and all the attention is now focused on the baby, and the team of first responders.

The adrenaline of the moment propels me forward and, before I know it, I'm in my cubby hole back at Martin's. The normalcy of the lunch rush and Habib's usual kitchen noise strikes me as surreal. In a trance, I make my way to the staff washroom and perform my usual pre-shift routine.

Then, reality hits. Returning to my cot, I reach under to loosen the floorboard that serves as my hiding place, and remove the bankroll I've accumulated over the past two years. I stash it in my backpack with my other belongings. I pass the kitchen area without as much as a glance towards Habib.

In the bar, I find Martin, rolling a keg into place beneath the bar. "Hey, Professor, how about a lunchtime beer?" he asks amiably.

I look at him and a feeling of guilt engulfs me as I betray my friend, "Look, Martin, I'm really sorry, but I can't do the afternoon shift today." I pause with internal conflict. "And maybe not tonight's shift either."

The smile is erased from his face instantly. "What's wrong?" he asks. "Are you in some kind of trouble?"

I try hard to smile, but even I can tell it's insincere. "No. No trouble. Nothing like that. There's just something I need to take care of."

Martin eyes me suspiciously, then, with resignation, he straightens up to his impressive size and says, "Well, that is a shame, man. You're not giving me good reason, and I'm not going to press you for more information. You know our deal. If you miss a shift, for any reason, we are done."

I think he expects me to spill the beans then, or at least reconsider and ask for a second chance, but I answer with as much dignity and respect as I can muster, "I know that, Martin, and I understand and respect your position. There is just something I have to do, and I can't explain it to you. I hope I'm not leaving you in a lurch."

Martin shakes his head, then holds out his hand and says, "Well... I guess this is goodbye then, Professor. Don't you worry about us. Habib will bitch about it, but you know I can have your job filled by tomorrow. You take care now, and, if the urge strikes you, come on by sometime. We're still friends, we can still enjoy a beer... don't you worry none."

I shake his hand and briskly walk across the restaurant and out the front door without looking back.

I make my way up Lafayette Street towards the

bus terminal, stopping on my way at the Buy Right Liquor Store to purchase a mickey of Jack Daniel's, which I tuck into my backpack. At the station, I scan the schedule and notice the next bus out is heading for Atlanta in ten minutes. It's roughly a five hour trip. Without hesitation, I make my way up to the ticket window and announce, "One way to Atlanta, please." I hand over the twenty-three dollars in fare, grab my ticket and take note that the bus is loading passengers at gate four. As my stay in Nashville began almost two years ago, now it ends in the same place. And I'm on my way again.

As I board the bus, I notice that it is very new. It has that 'new bus' smell, if that's a thing. The driver barely notices me as he scans my ticket. I make my way down the aisle, which has red carpet and is lined with small pin lights on the floor to compensate for the dim overhead light and dark tinted windows. There are very few passengers. I assume most people aren't happy about riding a bus on a hot summer day, but, reality is, this bus is environmentally controlled and possibly the most comfortable place I've been in a few years. I select a seat about three quarters down the length of the bus and park myself in the window seat. I slide my backpack under the seat, but not before removing the mickey of Jack Daniel's and stuffing it between the bus seat and the window with my spare tee shirt.

I'm in a half trance as I gaze out the window at nothing in particular, thinking of my hasty retreat from Nashville. I regret not having a chance to say goodbye to Travis and Jenny. They've been solid friends. It's been nice to see them carve out a life together, playing their music in the street and in various bars throughout the city. They even scraped enough together to rent a one bedroom apartment above a music shop, where they both work a couple of shifts a week to augment their performance earnings. I crashed a couple of nights there, but, given my unquenchable desire to get intoxicated every night, I tried not to make it a habit. While they never pushed me about my drinking, I think they also didn't wish to be enablers. I'm sure they also surmised that I have, at least in my own mind, a reason to drink. But to their credit, they never asked me to talk about it.

I will also miss my slacker friend, Jed. A gentle soul; I hope for his sake he finds his way in this world. While it's obvious he doesn't want to spend his life in his parents' basement, it's also obvious that he has no clue what to do with himself, college pipe dream aside. Perhaps witnessing me on occasion descend into the depths of alcoholic depression has given him some idea of what he *doesn't* want to do. He still enjoys weed and the occasional beer, but I've not seen him touch the hard stuff in a long time and he's said to me on many occasions, 'Man, that stuff is gonna' kill you...'. Perhaps, with any luck, he's right.

I'm in this state of mind and just thinking about how pissed Habib will be at my no-show for the afternoon shift, when I notice a small television above and to the left of the driver. It's tuned to the local news station. This is new to me; I've never seen a bus equipped with a live television feed. The banner at the bottom is what catches my eye. "Tourist bus passengers find overdose victim in Rosa Parks parking lot; rescue baby." As I read the banner, my attention shifts to the news story video. There is grainy footage, showing me, standing beside the car swinging wildly with my fisted Swiss army knife. It's surreal. In the last couple of years, those damn cell phones with video capabilities have become ubiquitous. There is no hiding anymore, even for someone as adept at hiding as I am.

The news anchor comes on and I strain to listen. What I do hear disturbs me. "The bus driver appeared to be the only witness who could speak English. Listen to what he had to say to our man on the spot, Rob Trawler." At that point, the grainy image is replaced with quality news footage. I recognize the bus driver, still sweating profusely from his run to the pay phone that summoned the ambulance. "Yeah, none of the passengers had phones that work in America...so I knew I had to find a pay phone, since my dispatcher was off on break and my phone was out of juice. I found one up at the corner and called 911, and by the time I got back some guy had bashed in the car window." The reporter breaks in at that point, "Is that man still here?" The driver looks a bit sheepish and says, "No. He just up and left as soon as the baby looked to be okay. I asked him his name and tried to get him to stick around. He just mumbled 'Brett Hull'... or something like that, and walked away." The reporter, Rob, at that point looks to the camera and says, "So there you have it. A mystery man, presumably named 'Brett Hull' saved the infant, who we cannot identify at this point, pending contact with next of kin. Unfortunately, the woman found in the driver's seat was pronounced dead at the scene, the apparent victim of an overdose. Back to you, Earl."

I pull my baseball cap further down, and sink into my seat, reaching for my Jack Daniel's. I take a long haul, and think about what I've just seen. It's inconceivable to me that I've been at the right place at the right time to intervene in potentially fatal situations for two innocent kids. But, that's what has happened. I don't know how to process this. Why is this happening? Why me, of all people? After what happened years ago.... it just doesn't make sense. And, I can't figure out how to feel about it. Then, as has been my habit for the past several years, the solution on how 'to feel about it' appears in my hand. I take another long pull from the Jack Daniel's, wishing I had bought a twenty-sixer. This mickey will be gone in no time.

The bus pulls into a truck stop at the halfway point to Atlanta. We are just outside of Chattanooga, at a place called Lookout Mountain. By now, the news channel from Tennessee has been replaced by a baseball game from Atlanta. The Braves are playing a rare afternoon game in sweltering heat against the Miami Marlins. Apparently, they are making up for a rain delay and will play a night game following the day game. For the umpteenth time, I hear the play by play guy intone, "I can't imagine where these young men are going to find the energy." In my semi-drunk state, the thought of throwing my empty mickey bottle at the television sweeps through my mind, but, as satisfying as that might be, I realize that it might draw some unwanted attention. Instead, I wait for the few passengers to file out, then grab my backpack and make my way to the door. The bus driver is hunched over his phone; he doesn't look at me as I descend the stairs but says in a monotone, "Bus departs in ten minutes." I nod, and alight to the gravel parking area. At the south end of the lot, some passengers are enjoying a scenic view. That doesn't interest me in the least. What catches my eye is the 'In and Out Convenience' store at the north end.

I amble over and enter the store and, to my relief, I see a bank of coolers with a selection of soft drinks and, more importantly, beer. I grab a tall boy of Sam Adams and continue my tour. The next aisle over I find what I'm looking for and seize a twenty-sixer of Jack Daniel's. I make my way to the counter, set my purchases down and rummage through my backpack for my bank roll.

At this point, the cashier looks at me and says with a southern drawl, "I'm sorry, sir, but in this state it ain't legal to sell liquor to someone who is already intoxicated. Perhaps you ought to find a quiet place to sleep it off."

I look up, and, for the first time, take note of the cashier. I see before me a dour young man of perhaps seventeen. His face is scarred with acne, and he sports a brush cut and braces. A trifecta of nerdism. His tee shirt, which hangs loosely from his gawky frame, has a UFO on display with the caption 'Mountain View is Out of This World' written across the chest. I look at him with no emotion, but continue to count out bills. Then, as calmly as ever, I say, "Listen, son, you don't want to do this. If you don't sell this to me now, I will be forced to come back here later, and at that point, I won't be in a mood to pay you. Do you understand what I'm saying, son?"

He looks hesitant, so I add, "Tell me, son, how often do the state troopers come through here? And where do you think the closest detachment is? Let's not make a big deal of this... just take my money and I'll be on my way."

Finally, he bags my purchases and accepts my cash. I say to him, "Keep the change."

As I'm leaving he blurts out, "No hard feelings, mister. Just doing what I thought was right."

I turn to him, "I know, son. But you know what? I've gotten into a lot of trouble doing what's right. Sometimes it's just not worth it."

I make my way back to the bus and surmise from the scowling look I get from the driver that I am the last to board. Before I take my seat, the bus lurches forward and I almost drop my precious cargo. I make for my seat and, once settled, open the tall boy. The beer is cold and refreshing, but I know it's just an appetizer. The main course remains in the paper bag for now.

The remaining two plus hours to the outskirts of Atlanta are uneventful. I take surreptitious swigs from my paper bag and, after a time, the familiar warm glow descends over me. My mind starts to wander as I watch the rural landscape gradually give way to suburban sprawl.

It's second nature for me to head to the downtown core, so I stay seated and watch as my fellow passengers disembark into the late afternoon heat, leaving the bus in various suburban outposts off of Interstate 75. Place names like 'Underwood Hills', 'Blandtown', 'Atlantic Station' soon transform to areas that offer more promise to me: 'Midtown', 'Old Fourth Ward', and finally 'Downtown'. There's only one other passenger on the bus, oddly dressed in a formal business suit and with a briefcase on his lap. He seems somewhat out of place travelling by bus and I idly wonder why he's not flying, taking Amtrak, or even renting a car to get to his destination. It dawns on me that, perhaps like me, something in his past has altered his life dramatically, and bus rides are all he can afford at the moment... perhaps he's had a DUI and lost his license... or, more sinister, perhaps he's doing penance for vehicular manslaughter. Who knows? Finally, beneath the gleaming glass of Atlanta's business district, he alights from the bus and I'm the lone passenger. I silently wish him luck in, what I've now determined in my drunk state, his job interview.

"What did you say, bud? Job Interview..?"

Perhaps I wasn't silent. The bus driver has

glanced over his shoulder with a familiar disapproving look. I murmur, "Nothing. Just let me out at the next stop please."

A few minutes later the brakes hiss, and the driver says unceremoniously, "End of the line, bud. Your stop. Corner of Martin Luther King and Forsyth."

I gather my backpack and quickly transfer my bottle of Jack, now dangerously close to empty, into the side pocket. As I begin to descend the stairs, the driver can't resist a parting shot. "Drunk at five o'clock. You're pathetic." As is my custom, I turn at the bottom of the stairs and, from street level, salute him with my middle finger as the door to the bus slams shut.

Why so judgemental? I think to myself, as I stumble forward, with no real destination in mind. Then I realize, he has a point. I am quite drunk. And, now that I'm no longer surrounded by the air conditioned comfort of the bus, I'm quickly turning into a sweaty foul smelling mess. This realization provides a temporary lucidity. Time for me to find shelter from this heat and humidity.

I take a closer look at my surroundings, and to my relief spot a sign across the street and less than a block from where I'm standing. "Underground Shops, Restaurants, Entertainment." I amble over and discover a large square dominated by paver stones interspersed with windowed pyramids and greenery. Signs indicating various store names, amusements, and eateries point to stairways, escalators and elevators. I've hit the motherlode, I think, smiling to myself. An underground shopping center. I can almost feel the relief as I quicken my pace towards the nearest entrance.

As I take the stairs down I can feel the heat slip away, and the noise of traffic surrounding the square is replaced with the soft hum of air conditioning, and of human activity. My eyes adjust to the lighting and I see before me a massive labyrinth of commercialism, and a stream of people crisscrossing from store front to store front, like bees in a hive. I have a minor panic attack. Encountering a crowd like this in an enclosed area is not something I enjoy, particularly when I'm drunk. I gingerly take the final steps down to the shopping concourse and search for the oasis I always seek in this type of situation. The men's room.

I wander slowly amongst the crowd, careful not to stumble into anyone. Despite my tactic to 'fit in' I'm still met with an occasional look of disdain. I realize I need to clean up quick or risk the ire of mall security. Finally, my eyes land on the generic man symbol, next to another symbol of a wheelchair. I make my way the next forty or so feet without incident and enter the modern tiled environment to the men's. I notice by the sign on the wall that 'Walter' had just cleaned the facility about ten minutes ago. The next scheduled time, based on the list of his previous appearances, is not for another fifty minutes. Perfect.

I check the stall for disabled users and note that unfortunately it doesn't include a sink, as some of the newer ones do. I'm slightly disappointed, but note that the washroom area appears to be kidney shaped, so that from the front of the washroom you can't see what is happening at the back. I make my way towards the back and see that, opportunely, that part of the room has a stall and sink, and is deserted. I strip down to my waist, then remove my spare socks from my backpack. It now seems like ages ago that my still-damp sock was used to comfort an overheated baby. I shake those thoughts from my mind and begin the process of making myself presentable. Holding one sock under the water I wet it and wring it out, then liberally apply hand soap. Wiping my face, I do my best to remove most of the sweat and grime, then repeat this process, working my way from top to waist, spending extra time around my armpits. After donning a clean tee shirt, I decide my balance is good enough to attempt washing my feet in the sink so I remove my shoes and socks. I roll up my left pant leg and put my foot in front of the faucet motion sensor. Leaning against the wall, I'm relatively steady. The water cascades over my foot, and I feel instant relief. I apply soap, rinse, and repeat the process with my right foot.

I take a brief rest and do a mental time-check, and realize that I've probably used up about twenty minutes of my time before Walter or one of his co-workers returns for the next round of cleaning. So far, I've only heard one or two other patrons enter the men's room, and nobody has ventured into the hidden nook I found at the back. With this in mind, I decide to chance one last cleaning exercise. I wet and soap a sock again, and make my way to the disabled user's stall. I gingerly remove my pants and underwear. I press the cool wet sock around my buttocks and genitalia. Nothing has felt so refreshing. I briefly consider making a quick shuffle out to a sink for a second round of genitalia bathing, but decide against it. Being naked in a men's room is not a particularly good strategy for someone keen on keeping a low profile. I remove the deodorant stick from my backpack and finish my grooming regimen. I then get dressed, replacing my sweaty undergarments and socks with fresh ones. I make my way back out to the sink where I wet and comb my hair, and brush my teeth. I also take the opportunity to quickly rinse and wring out my dirty clothes, stashing them in a plastic bag I find in one of the stalls. I feel confident that I can now blend in with the mall crowd.

Leaving the washroom feeling somewhat refreshed, I'm again thrust into the beehive of activity that is the mall. I spot an Information Center and amble over to look at the mall map. I realize that this is a massive complex, more than just retail outlets. I find my location at the 'You Are Here' marker. I'm in the middle of the shopping area, in the western-most part of the mall. As I explore the map, I find areas that may be more promising for my intentions. One is marked 'Museum', another, 'Entertainment', right next to 'Food Court.' Listening to the message my belly is sending to my head I decide to head to the food court, despite the thought that it will likely be well populated. That said, on my way there, I feel that my clean-up has worked:

I'm as invisible in the crowd as any shopper. I'm even given a nod by a mall cop, which for me is as good an indication of blending in as you can get. I arrive at the food court and I'm happy to see that it's only at about a quarter capacity – I guess this is too late for the lunch crowd and before the dinner crowd. The teenagers inhabiting the area couldn't care less about me.

I survey the various fast food and ethnic fare on offer and decide that the least offensive to my empty but fragile stomach would be Subway. I order a foot long tuna on white. Usually I stack subs with as many toppings as I can get, but this time I decide to stay away from anything that might trigger a worse hangover, so I stick with shredded lettuce and sweet pickles. I order a medium ginger ale to go with it and, after paying the bored teenager manning the till, make my way towards the museum area, hoping to find a quiet bench to eat and possibly grab a few winks.

I get slightly disoriented in the underground labyrinth, but eventually arrive in a quiet area that I assume is the museum. It appears this museum is mostly dedicated to Coca-Cola, and then I remember that Atlanta was the birth place of that particular syrupy soda brand. Early delivery vehicles, various signage and bottles and cans from the past in display cases are interspersed with interactive displays where disembodied voices narrate short video clips describing the manufacturing process or various 'historical figures' associated with Coca-Cola. Mercifully, the place is mostly deserted. It also has light that is turned towards

68

the displays and away from the traffic area, which to my immense satisfaction is dotted with comfortable benches. I find a bench nearest the least likely of the exhibits to garner interest – Coca-Cola at the 1996 Atlanta Olympics Games – and take a seat. I dig into my sub and, as hoped, it has a calming effect on my stomach. So much so, that I decide after drinking about a quarter of my ginger ale that I can mix the remainder of my Jack Daniel's with the remainder of my ginger ale. Just enough 'hair of the dog' to get me through the rest of the afternoon and, hopefully, send me off to slumber land. I finish my sub and wash it back with the remainder of my Jack and ginger. For the first time since I fled Nashville, I find myself mostly content and relaxed. I recline back in the bench and soon, my head begins bobbing, and I'm heading towards sleep.

I feel a slight stabbing in my ribs, and, rolling over, I blearily recognize the mall cop who nodded to me earlier. His Georgia drawl enters my consciousness. "Hey, fella. Sorry to interrupt your loitering, but the mall is closing in about five minutes and you can't sleep here tonight. You're gonna have to leave." This isn't delivered with any sort of derision, just factually and professionally. I've come to learn that there are two types of authority figures: those who recognize how petty it is to exercise that authority in most cases, and those who relish the opportunity to exercise their authority, no matter how pitifully small that authority may be. This mall cop is the former type, thankfully.

"Okay, man. I'm on my way," I say as I gingerly

roll over and stand up. Then, as I ponder my next move, I decide he is decent enough to ask him a few questions. "Hey, what time is it now?"

"Mall closes at 9 p.m."

"Oh, sorry. I slept longer than I meant to. Do you happen to know of any inexpensive lodgings in the area?" I think my manners and grammar surprise him. Not many homeless people use the term 'lodgings'.

He studies me for a moment and says, "Listen pal, you are in the high rent district here. You're not going to find anything for under two hundred a night. Can you afford that?"

I shake my head, "No chance."

"Okay then. Maybe you could try the Central Night Shelter on Washington Street." Pointing to his left, he adds, "Just exit over there, turn left onto Broad Street, then left again onto Martin Luther King, then right on Washington. You can't miss it."

"Thanks," I say, as I gather my backpack. Like I said, some authority figures are assholes, some aren't. This is one of the good guys.

"You're welcome. Enjoy your stay in Atlanta." And with that he tips his cap with his flashlight, and we part ways.

As I exit the mall I find the outside air has cooled and, combined with a half-decent sleep and a full stomach, and a bit of Jack and ginger, I feel almost human for the first time in a few days. The ten minute walk is actually refreshing. The scenery changes from urban commercial to pleasant civic buildings, mostly gothic style. Court houses, employment centers, and museums line a well treed boulevard. Amongst these is the Presbyterian Church that fronts the Central Night Shelter. It's an impressive structure. A sign points me down the side of the main building to a separate entrance with a sign that reads 'All of God's Children Welcome'.

Idly pondering whether God would consider me one of his children, I open the shelter door and peer inside. I'm confronted with a large multi-function space that appears to be in the process of turnover. Six or seven men – mostly black – are moving tables and chairs and replacing them with narrow blue foam mattresses, spread out about two feet apart on a floor that looks like it also serves as a gymnasium. A middle-aged man catches my eye, and, before I have a chance to retreat he speaks in a clear loud voice that demands everyone's attention, "Well, just don't stand there. Come on in and make yourself useful. We need help with these mattresses." A dozen eyes turn towards me, making it now impossible to back out. I enter the large space and, as instructed, join the gang and get to work laying mattresses.

Twenty minutes later, the task is complete. Tables and chairs are stacked neatly in a corner, replaced by about sixty mattresses spread across the floor. I'm still contemplating finding a place to settle amongst the civic buildings on Washington Street, instead of sharing this large space with fifty-nine others like me, when the man who appears to run the show approaches me and places a firm grip on my shoulder.

"What's your name, son?" he asks. It's then that I notice that the voice betrays the man in two ways. He is much older than I thought. I'm now guessing late seventies or early eighties, although you can't tell from his smooth black skin, or especially his grip. His voice also betrays his demeanour – while his words are gruff and loud, his eyes have a gentle glint to them. His dark eyes complement a hint of a smile on what appears to be his at-rest face.

Caught off guard by the juxtaposition of the voice and the man himself, I hesitate, then clear my throat and answer calmly, "Folks call me Professor."

"All right. Nice to meet you, Professor. You can call me Damon. Reverend Damon if you want to be formal, but I like Damon just fine. So, you need a place for the night?" He looks at me earnestly, and has caught me tongue-tied. While I do need a place for the night, I'm not ready to settle down just yet. I don't like the thought of spending the night sober.

"Umm. Yes, I'd like that. But I have to run a couple of errands first."

At this Damon shakes his head and lightly chuckles. "Oh, I know what kind of 'errand' you need to run. Okay, here's the deal. These doors are locked at midnight. You go ahead and run your errands, but if you don't make it back by then, don't bother to knock. You won't get in, and you won't be in anyone's good books. You clear?"

"Yeah,... uh, loud and clear," I stammer, like a

sixteen year old being told not to miss curfew.

"And one more thing", Damon continues, "Don't be bringing back anything that might tempt the others, if you catch my drift. We don't want any trouble here... and if you bring it, you won't be welcome back for a while. Now, go make some mayhem, if you must. I can tell you're itching to get out of here." And with that, he turns his back to me and moves on to another urban camper who has entered and who appears as disoriented as I did a few minutes ago.

I make my way back outside, where I find a few of my fellow mattress-layers congregating on the boulevard in the middle of Washington Street. As I approach and survey the situation, they lift their collective eyes wearily at me, and one of them, who I gather is their unofficial leader, tilts his chin at me and mutters, "What you looking at, cracker?"

Now, since my time as a traveller and urban camper, I've seen racial tension, but it is surprisingly rare. Most homeless people are more concerned with their next drink or high than they are about race relations. Sure, there is the occasional religious zealot or political conspiracy theorist who stirs up trouble, but race seldom causes friction amongst the street people. So, I'm caught off guard by this less than friendly greeting. Nonetheless, I keep approaching as I say in as non-confrontational way as possible, "I'm looking at you and your fellow homies... and hoping you can tell me where I might score some cheap liquor."

At this, I see his face change from one of

menace to a flicker of recognition. "Oh, wait. You the white boy just talking with Damon, right? We were wondering if you were some kind of hired help. You don't look like no drunk."

"I will take that as a compliment. But, I'm as hopeless a drunk as there is. And, I would really appreciate if you could help me find my next bottle. I'm approaching sober right now... and that's a problem for me." At this, the group of men all start to snicker, but, to my relief, not in a malicious way.

"Friend, you in the wrong part of town. We got libraries, court houses, churches... but we got no liquor round here. You gotta go about fifteen blocks south on Martin Luther King... then you find what you looking for."

"Well, I'm in the mood for a walk. Thank you, gentleman." I think I surprise them with my determination.

As I'm heading off, I hear one of them say to me, "You best be back by midnight." I wave in response and I hear more snickering. They don't think I will make it back, and they could be right. But I'll be damned if I'm going to spend the entire night sober.

It takes me a full forty minutes to find a liquor store, and with the heat and sobriety a film of sweat is now covering my body. The store is aptly named "My Friends Bottle Shop". I could certainly use a friend right now. As I scour the shelves, I find one of my best friends, Mr. Jim Beam, staring at me, right at eye level. My hands are shaking at this point. I take a fortyouncer and hastily make my way towards the cash register, stopping briefly on the way to grab a six pack of Budweiser conveniently cooling in the refrigerated section.

"That'll be thirty eight dollars," the uninterested evening clerk says. I hand him two twenties, barely managing to mumble 'keep the change' as I take a quick glance at the clock on the wall, and make a brisk exit. I pop a beer can and chug the whole thing down. That one was for cooling me off after my long walk as much as for kick-starting my sprint towards inebriation. Next, I twist the neck of my friend Mr. Beam and take a mighty slug of that sweet Kentucky bourbon. My body is soon enveloped in a mild wave of contentment. I take another long haul, then, slowly starting to calm down, assess my situation.

It is now after 11:30. I have absolutely no hope, or desire for that matter, to make it back to the shelter before midnight. My night out with my good pal Jim is just starting. That said, I did spot a few potential spots of interest on my way to My Friends Bottle Shop.

I pop another Bud and begin to retrace my steps. After about fifteen minutes of back-tracking through streets of mixed residential and commercial properties, I find myself at the edge of a large expanse of well treed greenery. I recognize this as the park I walked by earlier, just south of some major juncture of the city – possibly where Interstate 75 and Interstate 85 bisect the downtown area. I've never been fond of spending the night on a park bench, but I really can't stand waking up to the sound of early morning commuters blasting their horns and revving their engines, so given the choice between spending the night under an overpass by the highways and a bench somewhere in the park, I will take the park.

I wander through the park with some hesitation, as I'm vividly recalling an incident about three years earlier, in St. Louis. It was a dark night like this, with a new moon. I (of course) had been drinking and found myself on a park bench under a tree, thinking I would be hard to spot by anybody given the lighting, and also, should there be any rain, the tree would offer some shelter. I was wrong on the first count. I recall vividly the punch to my kidney that rudely awakened me. I rolled off the bench and groaned loudly, and was rewarded with a kick to the head and a terse 'shut up, drunk' rebuttal. I'd instinctively rolled up into a fetal position to ward off further blows, and was partially successful, only receiving one more painful kick to the ribs. The perpetrator's companion congratulated him on his aim, then said, 'Let's go, Willard. I think that'll be enough to keep this shit out of our park.' Laughing, Willard replied, 'You're right, Bart! My leg's a little tired from this shit-kicking anyway.' To punctuate this, Bart launched a solid gob of spit at me and said, 'Right, asshole?' 'Yes...I'm leaving,' I groaned painfully, then slowly rose to a semi-standing position and hobbled out of the park as fast as my battered body allowed.

So, this is mainly why I'm not fond of parks at night. At any length, I did learn a couple of lessons by that encounter. First, to avoid a beating, it's better to not stray too far from the lit paths. Find a bench not too deep in the park, preferably close to a side street with street lights. Assholes like Bart and Willard prefer to do their work in private, secluded areas. Second, when spending the night in a park, make sure you are deeply intoxicated. With that thought, I pulled heavily from Jim Beam's magic elixir. This at least kills some of the pain if nasty people decide they don't want you in their park.

Alternately sipping my Bud and gulping Jim Beam while stumbling around the periphery of the park, I find a suitable spot: a bench between two stands of small pine trees that is visible from the street and gently lit from a street light across the road. Perfect. I settle in with my backpack and toast my new surroundings by emptying my Jim Beam. The last lesson I learned from the Neanderthals Willard and Bart was to drink up while you can. You don't want to leave your dregs behind. I lose track of time and slowly descend into a deep drunken slumber.

"Hey, pal, shove over." I hear these words, and fail to register the significance. "I gotta rest these weary bones, and feed my pigeons." I roll over, and, as my eyes adjust to the morning light, I see a slight woman with mousy brown hair streaked with grey, staring at me expectantly and gesturing with her hands.

I slowly yield part of the bench as I sit upright. I have a taste of copper and bile in my mouth and my stomach is turning, but, despite this, I try to be courteous. "I'm sorry, ma'am, I didn't mean to monopolize the whole bench. I suppose I slept longer than planned."

As a flock of pigeons approach, cooing softly, she turns to me and says, "Well, I suppose you did sleep in. It's going on half past eight. Don't you have a job to go to?" I'm surprised she has mistaken me for a working man, and equally surprised at how early it is. That said, I'm not in much of a mood to engage her further in conversation.

"You are right. I must be going."

As I slowly gather myself and my backpack and start to shuffle away, I hear her say, "And don't you worry about your empties. I get the refunds, and that pays for my pigeon feed." I turn back and take another look. She has a Cheshire cat grin that I can't help but return.

"See you," I say without committal.

"Sure," she says with that grin.

I slowly make my way back to the shelter, and once again, I'm confronted by the same group of men who had congregated on the boulevard last night. "Hey, look what the cat dragged in," their ring-leader crows to the delight of his followers. "You look like shit, cracker," he says with a twisted smile.

"I feel like shit, too" I respond to hoots of laughter.

"Well, what did sister Damon tell you? Back by midnight or you be camping out. Looks like you camped out."

I nod and shuffle over to the door of the shelter without further comment. As I enter, Damon spots me and nods. He knows the look.

He ambles over and says, "Grab a tray, we have the basic breakfast here until 10 a.m." I do as instructed and he guides me through the process while making light conversation.

Curious, I ask him, "So what's with those guys who seem to help out here, but hang out on the boulevard most of the time?"

Damon shakes his head. "That would be Rudy and his crew. They sell drugs and whatnot to whoever's buying. They do help out on occasion so that I don't blow the whistle on them for loitering. I also make sure they don't get too aggressive with their sales, if you know what I mean."

I look at him as we make our way to a fold out table. "Keep your friends close and your enemies closer," I say.

"Amen to that," he replies.

Atlanta to Jacksonville, January 2010

After spending several months in the fair state of Georgia, I have a fairly regular routine. Most days I'm awakened by the pigeon lady, who I now know is named Doris. She is very kind, and often has a cup of coffee for me. Doris is a widow who lives very close to the park on Kelly Street. She has become somewhat of an intermediary between me and the collection of elderly people who live in her neighborhood. Do you need your lawn cut? Your hedge trimmed? Some eves troughs cleaned? Screens repaired? A drain unplugged? No problem. Doris will arrange that with the Professor. In exchange, people pay me in cash or kind. Some have clued in to the fact that, besides being an urban camper, I'm also a functioning alcoholic and they will actually hand me a six pack of beer for a job well done. Call it enabling if you want, but I think they are just being practical. They are like Doris: just happy to have someone to help them out and to chat with. This handy-man work has been just enough to support my needs, which are modest.

After Doris and I have our morning chit chat and she tells me about the latest job she has me lined up to do, I head over to 'My Friends Bottle Shop' and purchase a couple of tall boys and some jerky, for a meal I refer to as 'brunch'. I then do the odd job thing, which generally takes no more than a few hours, and return to the bottle shop to purchase a twenty-sixer of whatever hard liquor is on sale. I usually down about half the bottle by 5 p.m., then head over to the Central Night Shelter. I hide my bottle in my backpack, have dinner at the shelter and help Damon clean up and ready the space for the nightly guests. Seldom do I actually stay at the shelter, since I still have a half bottle of cheap liquor to consume and that is frowned upon for sleepovers. Sometimes, I will buy some weed from Rudy, but mostly I stay out of his way. I often return to the bottle shop for a few more tall boys or a mickey if I'm feeling in need of some extra stimulation. So, I think of my days in terms of the three 'Ds': Doris, Drinking, Damon. It's simple. It's easy. It's the private life I'm always seeking.

I've added a bit of weight to my backpack to accommodate my handy-man work... an adjustable wrench, a hammer, a multi-head screw driver, and pliers. That's about as complicated as my life has become.

And then, my quiet existence amongst the elderly and homeless of Atlanta is interrupted. It happens again.

Doris sends me to her friend Annette's house. She lives a few blocks east on Park Avenue, past the fire house. Annette is somewhere between sixty and seventy, divorced. She has that sinewy look of a tough old bird who has seen it all. Tanned, bleached blond, with a chain smoker's voice. I've been to her place a few times and it has always struck me that Annette looks and sounds very much like so many of the homeless women I've met over the years, only she isn't a raging alcoholic or a drug abuser. She looks after her granddaughter Emmaline while Emmaline's parents are at work. Emmaline is a cute little charmer, who, whenever I see her at Annette's, proudly declares 'I'm flee' which I take to mean she is proud to be three years old.

Annette greets me at the door. "Hello, Professor. So good you could come."

"Hi, Annette. What can I do for you today?"

"Well, the thing is, I'm hearing this funny noise coming from the basement. I know, basements are unusual here in Atlanta but this old house has one. Day before yesterday I went down there and saw I had about a quarter inch of water on the laundry room floor. I cleaned it all up, but yesterday there was more. I'd like to know what's happening, and if you can fix it. Can you take a look?"

I head downstairs into the unfinished basement and as my eyes adjust to the semi darkness, I spy through a doorway the washing machine and tub against the far wall. At my request Annette provides a flashlight, hopefully allowing me to avoid a worsening headache from straining at the dim light.

My first thought is that maybe the discharge pipe from the washer isn't pointed into the tub, or something has sprung a leak. On inspection, I find neither to be the case. As I start to inspect the seal around the laundry tub drain, my attention is caught by an odd high-pitched mechanical whining noise behind me. My eyes are drawn to the corner, where I see a vertical pipe that makes its way up from a hatchway on the floor and disappears into the ceiling joists. I make my way over and open the hatchway lid, and, peering down with the flashlight, I believe I've found the source of the noise and perhaps the water issue. There is a sump pump nestled in an old laundry tub that has been inserted into a hole in the floor. The pump is completely surrounded by silt. The weird noise is the pump trying to clear ground water that has gathered below the house's foundation, but instead of clearing water it is getting 'suffocated' with all that silt.

I return upstairs and give Annette the news. "The good news is, I found the problem. You have a sump pump that is plugged up."

Annette looks at me like I'm from another planet. I briefly explain the issue. "Oh, that's what that little door on the floor was for. Oh... look at me, I'm a poet," she laughs. Since basements and sump pumps are both somewhat of an anomaly in Atlanta, I understand Annette's confusion. "What needs to be done to fix it?"

"Well, the bad news is, I'm not certain. But what I will do is clean out all this silt and then pour a pail or two of water in and see if the pump still works. I'm afraid if that doesn't work, you will need a plumber, and you may need to replace the pump." She directs me to go continue while she puts Emmaline down for her nap.

With that I go to work and after an hour and a half the silt is cleared away and disposed of in the back

83

gardens. I test the pump with water, and it looks like it's going to be okay. I call Annette down to show her what I've done, and how the sump pump is now working.

"It looks like cleaning out your sump pump has worked, and mission is accomplished. The thing is, I don't know how long it will take before the silt might become an issue for you again."

"Oh, I wouldn't worry about that. I've been divorced for over forty years now and I'm pretty sure that useless lout I married never gave that pump a single thought. I reckon it took fifty years for that much muck to get in there. Thank you for your help, Professor... let's go back upstairs and I'll get my wallet to pay you." She heads upstairs while I finish tidying up.

I don my ever-present backpack, and as I'm about to make my way back upstairs, I hear sudden ear piercing shrieks coming from the direction of the kitchen. I sprint up the stairs and find Annette cradling her unconscious granddaughter on the kitchen floor. "She got into something, over there by the sink! She was just retching, but now's she's not even moving! Oh my God! She's going to die!"

I look at Emmaline, who has turned a greyish pale blue colour and has redness forming under her eyes. I take in the spilled pink liquid on the kitchen floor by the sink, alongside an open mason jar. "Okay, Annette, don't worry, I'll take her to the fire station up the street! I'm sure there'll be a paramedic there." I say this as I snatch Emmaline and race out of the house, leaving Annette with a dazed look on her face.

Atlanta Fire Station number 10 is one block from Park Avenue. I've never run as fast as this in my life and, as I arrive at the station, firefighters washing a fire truck in the driveway have the wherewithal to recognize my distress. They quickly see why I'm distressed, with Emmaline hanging limply in my arms. "Let's get her to the paramedic," one shouts. "This way!"

We hustle into the station to the paramedic truck, and Emmaline is quickly placed on a gurney. Without thinking I jump into the ambulance beside her and as we launch out of the station for the hospital the paramedic puts an oxygen mask on Emmaline while asking me, "What can you tell me?"

"I think she ingested a toxic pink liquid that was kept under the kitchen sink. Not sure what it was." Before the words are out of my mouth, the paramedic is finding a vein and taping a saline drip line onto Emmaline's little arm. He takes her blood pressure and heartrate, asking, "How long since she ingested the liquid?"

Thinking back to my last conversation with Annette in the basement, but uncertain of what Annette was doing before that, I realize I don't really know. I reply, "I'm just not certain."

He utters, "She's stable at least. We are about ten minutes from the hospital. The driver is radioing ahead and will bring them up to speed. It's too soon to be sure, but given her vitals I think she's going to be okay. "

I breathe a hopeful sigh of relief and we continue our ride in silence as he continues to monitor little Emmaline. When we reach the hospital, we are greeted by emergency staff who hustle Emmaline out of the vehicle and into Emerg. As I hop out, adrenaline still pumping, I hear the paramedic reporting her vitals. I stand back, uncertain what to do next.

The paramedic turns back to me, "I think you saved that little girl's life. Please come with me to admittance, and then I'd like to buy you a coffee," he says with a big smile, clapping me on the back.

It's then that I realize that, once again, I've put myself in an awkward situation. "Umm, okay. Thanks. But really, it was nothing; you're the hero here."

He's ushering me towards the admittance desk, so I have to think fast. "Look, I'm not related to that little girl. I'm a nobody. A drunk, actually... and very much in need of a drink. You have to talk to her grandmother. Her name is Annette... she's at 78 Park Avenue."

As I say this, I hear a plea coming from the emergency entrance and I recognize Annette's raspy calls of terror. "Where is she? Is she all right?"

As we approach, I reassure her, "Annette, she's okay. They think she's going to be fine."

"Oh, Professor, I can't thank you enough. I don't know what I would've done if you hadn't been there to help little Emma." She breaks down in tears, and blinking hard, I feel my eyes welling up too. Then

I'm brought back to reality by the paramedic who has lingered beside us.

"Professor... what? You are a hero, and I want to make sure you get acknowledgement for your actions today. A civic award. Lemme get the wheels in motion. What's your name, pal? "

"Uh, yeah, it's, ah, David Legwand."

"Legwand?" he inquires, "That's an interesting surname; doesn't sound local."

"Well, I'm originally from Nashville. We have a lot of weird names there. Ever heard of Conway Twitty?"

The paramedic laughs, and turns to Annette. "You're the grandmother, right? Let's go over to admittance and you can give them the info on this little girl." He starts to walk her towards the admittance desk, turning his back to me.

And, with that, I fade into the background and quietly slide out the door. Luckily in all the commotion I've managed to keep my backpack with me. I catch the bus that conveniently pulls up out front at that moment, and I head back into the heart of Atlanta. I know I have to beat it out of town, but first I have to figure out how.

The bus stops at its first station – Jesse Hill Jr – after leaving Grady Memorial Hospital. It just happens to be located right across the street from the Georgia State Marta train station. As Damon would say, 'The Lord works in mysterious ways'.

I enter the station, and I'm immediately

87

confronted with a row of retail chain stores lining the walls of the station, including a liquor store. Ha, today is my lucky day, I think, ironically. I rush through the aisles, then to the counter with a twenty-sixer of Jack Daniel's, pay the man and make my way to the Marta ticket wicket. Next train is to Jacksonville, leaving in five minutes from track six. I purchase a one way ticket.

I take my seat and as the train pulls out of the station, I take a long slow haul of Jack. The entire time that has elapsed from hospital departure to train departure is no more than twenty minutes. I congratulate myself on my very fortunate timing and logistics, as I take another haul of Jack. But then, I think to myself, 'How has this happened to me again, and how is it possible that everything just seemed to line up like it did? Really, what the hell is going on here?!'

Part Two

"How people treat you is their karma; how you react is yours." – Wayne Dyer

St. Louis, January 2010

I stare at my laptop with a dispassionate gaze. It has been weeks (months?) since my last feature story. My editor, the abrasive and shrewd Tony Fallows, is also aware of my lack of productivity and is not shy about reminding me.

"Joanne. Wake up! You aren't getting paid to stare at your laptop all day. I'm already on thin ice with Randal. I need something for the winter edition, or we both could be out of a job." Randal is in reference to Jerome Randal, our publisher and owner. Tony thinks that Jerome is obsessed with deadlines and so, therefore, we all should be obsessed with deadlines. But I know that what Jerome is actually concerned about is a certain editor who does little to hide his contempt for print media (i.e. Tony). Tony fancies himself a blogger and has played fast and loose with the interpretation of his contract. He has been posting articles under a pseudonym for over a year now, breaching the intellectual property clause of his contract with Jerome.

Jerome is actually a patient man. As the publisher of our little boutique publication, the 'Atlantic Quarterly', he has to be. In what has become a rarity in the print business, Jerome understands that some stories need to percolate. He pays investigative journalists like myself to sniff out stories, then dig deep to fill out the whole picture for our medium sized, but dedicated readership. My last story took a full four months to develop. While Tony verbally abused me daily with diatribes about publishing deadlines and his favourite phrase 'time to monetize' (which he explained is his way of saying, 'your writing needs to make money now'), Jerome would simply ask where I was in the investigation, then nod approvingly and say 'keep digging'.

As it turned out, my digging did turn up the unsavoury truth of a teen 'sex slave' prostitution ring which was being aided and abetted by a local councilman, his partner, and the vice squad of the local police force. It was an in-depth report that led the FBI to arrest and charge all of the key players, including a minor who was actually the main recruiter for the ring. Fargo, North Dakota is still reeling. I was nominated for a Pulitzer, affording me the luxury of 'staring at my laptop all day.'

So, Jerome Randal has my back. I think it also doesn't hurt that he appears to be smitten with me. I'm not ashamed to admit, I'm willing to use that to my advantage. At 42 years old, I'd call myself attractive (not to brag). I'm five eight, 130 pounds. My legs are toned and long, and, my breasts have only been modestly impacted by gravity. I've kept my waist line slim, due more to a good metabolism than any workout regimen. A stylish cut and dye job keeps my stark black hair out of my face, which (touch wood) is still free of wrinkles. My green eyes round out the look that, I've

91

heard through the grapevine, some men refer to as the 'Irish Goddess.' I take it as a compliment. At any rate, I like to think Jerome values me more for my work than my looks, but, it doesn't hurt my cause that both are valued. And, Jerome is no fool. He is aware of Tony's extracurricular activities and, I suspect, has me in mind to succeed Tony as editor.

I continue scrolling though the Associated Press wire service, when a headline catches my eye. "*Mystery man saves toddler from poison*". I read the dateline. 'Atlanta, January 13'...so... two days ago. The article:

"*Police are looking for a man who*

identified himself as 'David Legwand from

Nashville' in connection with a paramedic

emergency that happened on Park Avenue

around 2 p.m. Tuesday. A toddler, who will not

be identified for privacy reasons, was brought to

the fire station by Legwand, and then was

rushed to Grady Memorial Hospital by

paramedics, where she was treated for

consumption of a toxic substance.

"*The guy is a hero*", *stated paramedic*

Mike Rogers. "We weren't called to the address, and in this case that is likely why the little girl is still alive. He ran her the block or so from the home to our station, and told us that she had swallowed something toxic. That's all the information we needed to stabilize her and get her into Emerg as quickly as possible. If he hadn't run her here, it would have taken us at least fifteen minutes to scramble and fight our way through traffic to get to her. I just wish he would have stuck around."

Due to Legwand's disappearance, police are treating this as potentially suspicious, although the grandmother, who can also not to be named, was emphatic in her praise of Legwand's actions. "I was in shock, watching my granddaughter retching and unconscious, when he just picked her up and started running

with her, yelling...' I'm going to the fire station'.

At first I didn't know what was going on.... Then

I figured it out. You should have seen him run.

He was like an Olympic sprinter. I never got a

chance to thank him properly, as he just

disappeared from the hospital and I haven't

seen him since."

When approached to elaborate on his

suspicions, Police Detective Murray of Atlanta

Central Division simply said, "Whenever there is

a life threatening event like this, especially

involving children, we like to speak to all the

witnesses. I ask that Mr. Legwand comes

forward to give a statement, or, if anybody can

help us locate him, they contact me at the

precinct."

I roll this around in my head. The story sounds somewhat familiar. Then it strikes me. I do a search using the search bar at the top of the Associated Press website. Key words, 'toddler saved'. Wow. Over forty thousand hits. I should not be surprised. Stories like this are gold for local beat reporters, and I realize my mistake. I need to be more specific.

I hover over the button to 'refine search' and click. The options appear. I decide to start with the prior year, and so I select 'Date' and fill in 'Start Date' of January 1 2009, 'End Date' of December 31 2009. Wow. Over four thousand hits. We have a lot of accident prone toddlers in this country apparently. I realize this isn't going to be as easy as I thought it would be, and settle in to do more selective searching. I decide to search each quarter, systematically, starting with January 1 to March 31.

Finally, in the third quarter, with my patience running thin after scanning close to three thousand headlines, "Eureka!" I shout, still hunched over my laptop.

"What?" Tony looks at me through his office door, a look of mild irritation on his slightly red, slightly puffy face.

"Nothing... yet," I respond. "Sorry, I'm just working on a hunch and I may have found something. But I'm not ready to share just yet."

"Fine," Tony harrumphs, "But... I hope you are

in a sharing mood soon, and that I will be the first person you share with."

After that brief exchange, I open up the article attached to the headline *"Drifter disappears after rescuing baby from car."* The dateline reads *"Nashville, August 12 2009"*

"A man, in his mid to late 30s, sporting

a backpack, came to the rescue of a baby boy

trapped inside an overheated car. The child was

left in peril when an unidentified women,

assumed to be his mother, apparently died of an

overdose at the scene. A scene that one

eyewitness described as 'devastatingly sad'.

Sid Ferraro, a bus driver with a tour

company explains, "I was picking up passengers

at our designated parking lot, to take them for

an overnight gambling junket. I noticed a bunch

of them freaking out and pounding on this late

model Ford. At first I couldn't figure out what

was going on, since none of them spoke a word

of English. Then I got closer and I see this dead

woman... maybe early twenties, in the front

seat. But, even worse, I see this baby in a car

seat in the back seat turning beet red, with his

tongue rolling out of his mouth. It was very hot

that day, and it appeared the baby was dying of

the heat inside the car. I couldn't believe my

eyes."

Ferraro then explains how he left the

scene to get emergency responders. "My cell

phone was out of juice, and my dispatcher was

on break, and none of the tourists had local cell

phone service, so I had to find a pay phone. I

found one down the street and called 911 and

then ran back to the bus. By the time I got

there, the baby was out of the car and being

looked after by a couple of the tourist ladies.

97

But this one guy, I'd say roughly 35 give or take, looking kind of rough around the edges, is being circled by a bunch of the tourists, being congratulated, having his picture taken and his hand shaken. I asked the guy if he was the one that rescued the baby from the car and he just kind of shrugged, but I could tell from the people shaking his hand that he must have been. Then, as we hear the ambulance approaching, he seems to get all kind of twitchy. The next thing I know, he's vanished. I managed to get a name though, he said he was Brett Hull, just visiting from St. Louis."

The infant is being treated at HCA Healthcare and he is expected to recover fully from what doctors described as heat stroke symptoms.

Police are treating the death of the

young woman, whose name is being withheld

pending notification of next of kin, as an

unintentional drug overdose. However, they

would like to speak with Hull to complete their

investigation. Anyone who may know him or his

whereabouts are asked to contact Nashville

Police."

The article is accompanied by a shadowy photo of the hero. As noted by the bus driver, he looks to be about 35 to 40, and a bit rough around the edges. I'd also say he's handsome in a rugged kind of way, but what really strikes me is the look on his face. There is a slight hint of panic that just doesn't seem to jibe with someone being described as a hero. Perhaps it's the adrenaline he's feeling at that moment. Regardless, it's hard to ignore the parallels between these two stories. Both involve a mystery man, who happens to be Johnny-on-the-spot when there is an infant or toddler to be saved. My ingrained sense of cynicism gained from years of working for the fifth estate smells something fishy.

But there is more. Two times can be a coincidence, but, while my memory isn't as sharp as it used to be, I do recall some things. And, in my gut I'm certain this isn't just a coincidence, just as certain as I am that there is a third, similar, story that I recall reading a couple of years ago. Which means I have more digging to do.

The meeting is held in Tony's office. This is his way of projecting that he's in control. I'm there, dressed to the nines as they say, as is our benefactor, Jerome, who has taken note of my efforts. As my mother used to say, 'There is no shame in using your God-given talents'.

I get much of my world view from my mother, Patsy. She was an attractive woman and knew it. For her, this was both a blessing and a curse. A blessing in that she could get just about any man she set her sights on; a curse because she did not have much luck in picking them. And, while it may sound sexist, picking a man was important for my mother given her time and place.

Patsy grew up as an only child in rural Idaho near the town of Ketchum, population now around 3,400. It was – and still is – a sleepy little village relying mostly on tourism to keep its economy going. Her father managed a hotel where her mother also worked cleaning rooms. Given their hours of work, as a kid my mom often returned from school to an empty house. As she grew into her teens, she became more independent. She learned quickly that she could parlay her looks and independence into dates with men who would buy her nice meals and drinks.

Patsy met my father, Chad, while he was on a March break vacation at Sun Valley, the local ski destination. According to mom, Chad was smitten the first time he laid eyes on her. After a whirlwind romance (that culminated in my conception) Chad returned to Idaho State University where he was a sophomore. Unfortunately, in my mom's second trimester, Chad was killed in an automobile accident. To make matters worse, when I was about fifteen months old, both of my grandparents were diagnosed with a rare form of pancreatic cancer that took both their lives barely one week apart, right before my second birthday. I later found out that the hotel they worked in was the cause of a 'cancer cluster' linked to a contaminated well. Of course, by the time I found this out, the hotel had been torn down and the owners had passed away, their meagre estate long settled. So, the long and short of it is, Patsy was a 19 year old single mom with a high school education living in a small town. She knew her best path to any sort of economic stability was to find a man who could help provide for her and me.

As I got older and observed my mom going through a string of relationships, I learned some lessons. The first, and by far most important lesson was to NOT become dependent on another person, financially or emotionally. The second lesson I learned was to not be afraid to use your looks and charm to influence how others perceive you. The nuance here is that their perception of you will often dictate how they treat you as a person. I want to be clear, my mom Patsy believed, and I now too believe, that it is not manipulative if people act on their own perceptions. My mom finally found a good man and settled down, so the last lesson that I learned from my mom was that perseverance and patience pay off.

At any rate, sitting in Tony's office, I'm not here to flirt. I'm here to persevere and to patiently pitch my story. It took a while, but my research has paid off.

Tony begins, "So, Joanne, you missed our last quarterly, and, barring a miracle, you might miss this one too. I really hope all that time staring at your laptop has paid off. What do you have for us?"

Before I respond, Jerome interjects, "Now, Tony. I know you have our quarterly's best interests at heart, but, we have a Pulitzer nominee here. I think we should give her as much rope as she needs."

My cue. "Thank you, Jerome. And Tony... if you don't like what you hear, then you get to be the one who throws the rope over the tree branch and starts pulling. Trust me, I know my stuff."

"Fine. Let's go then. What have you got?"

"What I have, gentlemen, is either a cross-country spree of heroism, or one very sick puppy. Either way, I think it could be a hell of a story." I explain in some detail the three separate stories that I've discovered – first one in St. Louis in September 2007, then Nashville in August 2009, then, most recently in Atlanta in January 2010. In each case, a young child is saved from a life-threatening event by a rough-looking mystery man who vanishes from the scene just as quickly as he appeared. Local police are left with questions, but can never follow up, since our mystery man, who is generally regarded as a hero, seems to be very media shy. He..."

Tony interjects, "Okay, I grant you, this could be an interesting story, but isn't it a bit hard to believe these heroes are all the same guy? After all, as you said... these events happened in different states, several months or years apart from each other. It's a big country. Is it so hard to believe that we are looking at isolated incidents?"

Tony has a smug look on his face. And, make no mistake, this isn't his 'at rest bitch face' as my pal Judy described it once. It's smugness. Like I'm his student and he just caught me cheating on a test. Nonetheless, I hold it together and decide to turn the tables a bit on Tony.

"Tell me something, Tony. Do the names Gordon Howe from Detroit, Brett Hull from St. Louis and David Legwand from Nashville mean anything to you?" I ask, widening my eyes and batting my eyelashes in a very innocent sort of way. I'm enjoying this way too much.

"No, should they?" he asks.

I answer, "They are the aliases that our mystery man used."

He doesn't get it. "Aliases? How do you know that? Your point is..?"

Got you, sucker, I think, as I lower the boom. "Actually, those names belong to ice hockey professionals. All had very distinguished careers in the cities noted. Now, Tony... what do you think the odds are of three different men in various states, each saving a child, then providing an NHL All Star's name as their own?"

Jerome laughs. "Pretty miniscule, I'd venture. This could be big, Joanne. Take whatever time and resources you need to bring it home."

Tony turns fifty shades of red. I fail to suppress a massive smile that some might say looks like gloating. Tony can't help himself. "Well I hope you can do so by our March cut-off date."

I smile benignly. "Sure boss. I'll try my best." The perfect non-committal answer. Tony glares. Jerome smiles.

Oh, this is going to be fun, I think to myself.

It was a difficult decision to make. How should I start my investigation into our mystery man? Some in law enforcement might say I'd be wise to start with the most recent sighting in Atlanta. But, I'm not law enforcement... I'm a journalist. So, my instinct says start at the beginning. Chronologically that means St. Louis. This also makes sense to me because it's likely that our hero (or villain... to be determined) wasn't actually from St. Louis. Where did he actually come from? Is he homeless? What's his background? What's his connection (if any) to that first child he 'saved' in St. Louis?

The other thing that compels me to start in St. Louis is that the story in question is now well over two years old. Locating and talking to people who recall the story will become more difficult the longer that time stretches.

For the flight to St. Louis, I'll wear my black power pantsuit, with an off white silk blouse and my three inch heels. The power suit will be useful once I land, to conduct my first interviews. On this point, St. Louis is a good place to start for yet another reason: I happen to have an ongoing semi-professional and personal relationship with a local reporter (it's complicated). My plan is to talk to the local reporters who covered the story of the drowning toddler, law enforcement, and, if I can track her down, the mother of the child who was saved.

I pack light for the trip I'm hoping will take no more than four days, fitting everything nicely into my red carryon: hygiene bag (always sitting ready for a trip), underwear, an extra pair of jeans, warm socks, a couple of long sleeved tee shirts, fleece, windbreaker, empty backpack, hiking boots, and a sports bra. Once I have the stories of those immediately connected to the story, I plan on spending time amongst Mr. Gordon Howe's peer group, who are likely the homeless of St. Louis. Power suit off; hiking clothes on.

The flight is uneventful and we land on schedule

at Lambert International Airport. It's midday, so I'm in luck – I should beat the rush hour traffic. I hail a cab and ask the cabbie to take me to the St. Louis Post-Dispatch building on Tenth Street North. Without a word, the cabbie jolts the late model Impala from the curb and in minutes we are cruising on Interstate 70 heading south. As we're driving, I thumb through my contacts and find the guy I want to see first.

On the third ring, I'm greeted by his message: 'You've reached Darren Crowley of the Post-Dispatch. If this is regarding an editorial I penned that you didn't like, hang up because I don't care. Otherwise, leave a message and God willing, I might return your call.' Good ole' Darren. Clearly he's made lots of friends with his opinionated views. I leave a message. "Hi Darren, it's Joanne. I'm in your neck of the woods and hoping you can give me a leg up on a story I'm working on. I'm on my way to your office, so please call me back or I will make a scene when I arrive." That should get his attention. Ten minutes later my cell rings. I note the caller on call display. "Hello, Darren. How thoughtful of you to return my call."

"You didn't leave me much choice. The last thing I need in the office is a scene. I can picture it now, you claiming I'm a dead beat dad... or maybe a defrocked priest that had his way with you... or a carny that impregnated you then skipped town once the 'tilt-a-whirl ' romance was over. Nope, I won't be giving you that satisfaction. I will meet you in the lobby. When do you think you'll get here?"

106

A brief exchange with my cabbie and I respond, "Ten minutes, max."

"You don't fool around do you? You want to tell me what this is about?"

"No, not really. I'd prefer to wait and talk in person. That way, I'll know if you're lying or not."

Darren and I have a history. We both studied journalism at NYU. Over the course of several semesters we became a bit more than just classmates. It's the same old story. You get comfortable with a group of like-minded individuals, then, suddenly, seemingly out of nowhere, you find yourself being looked at differently in the group. Suddenly, they don't see you as an individual anymore. They see you as part of a sub-group within the group. A couple. That's what we were: 'a couple'. I still find it hard to explain, and yet, there was and still remains an undeniable attraction. Did we have sex? Sure. I mean, I wasn't a nun in college, and Darren was/is pretty cute. Did we hang out a lot together? Sure. Like I said, we were part of an extended group of like-minded individuals. Everyone in our crowd had the same classes at NYU, the same places to hang out, mostly the same thoughts on sex, love, politics, religion. It was fun. It was comfortable. And then, suddenly, it wasn't.

Towards the end of our graduating year, we could both feel a strain on the relationship. It seemed every time we went out with our pack of marauding journalism students, Darren and I would end the evening with an argument. It always terminated with him saying something like, 'Well it's pretty obvious that you don't feel about me the same way that I feel about you'. Then I'd try to mollify him by saying that wasn't true. But, really, it was true... sort of. Darren wanted commitment; Darren wanted stability; Darren wanted us to be exclusive. Darren even talked about kids. I didn't want any of those things, then.

Everything came to a head one evening just before the end of the school year. The plan was to meet up with a bunch of our friends in Lincoln Park, then cab uptown for a night of cocktails and dancing. I arrived at our meeting spot on time and found it deserted. I was a bit confused, checked my phone for text updates but found nothing. Five minutes later, Darren showed up sporting the widest grin I had seen on his face in weeks. He sat down beside me on the park bench I had sequestered and, registering the look on my face, started by saying, 'I guess you've figured out that it's just us tonight'.

'I did notice that I've been sitting here alone, and no one but you has arrived, so yes...,' I dryly replied.

'Well, there's a good reason for that. I wanted us to be alone tonight.'

I could feel a pit forming in my stomach. That look on his face. The careful orchestration of the moment. I knew what was coming before it happened.

'So, you know that job I interviewed for as the local beat writer at the St. Louis Post-Dispatch? Well, I got it. Which brings me to this.' At this point, he reached into his satchel and pulled out a small box, which he opened to reveal a diamond engagement ring. 'Come with me, Joanne. Marry me, and come with me to St. Louis.' He gushed this last part, and my heart skipped a beat.

It doesn't matter that I knew it was coming. To this day, I can't explain what I did. I don't consider myself a mean person. I cry at sad movies. I love kittens and puppies. And he really did look like a puppy at that moment. But, instead of gently letting him down or hugging him and telling him *how beautiful the ring is and how unexpected it all is... and oh gee-whiz... it's overwhelming, let me think about it.* Nope. I laughed. I laughed right in his face and said, 'Are you crazy? I can't marry you, Darren! I can't marry anyone right now. I'm about to graduate and start a real life. One where I make money. Make new friends. Live alone for a while. You want me to forget all that and become what... some suburban housewife in St. Louis?' I crushed him, right on the spot. For the next few weeks I backtracked a bit, consoling him, telling him the truth. It wasn't him. It was me. I just wasn't ready. Maybe we could try a long distance relationship. But we both knew it was over. Or, at the very least, it was on indefinite hold.

And now, fast-forwarding to present day, after a decade of exchanging Christmas cards, the occasional catch-up phone call, and getting drunk with each other at the weddings of mutual friends, we are about to have our first real professional conversation. And my goal will be to keep it that way. Professional. But, like I said... it's complicated.

As per our brief phone exchange, Darren meets me in the lobby of the Post-Dispatch building. Not one for small talk, he takes a glance at the carryon suitcase I've got with me and starts in. "Please tell me you have a place to stay, Joanne, because I don't think my current girlfriend Trish would be onside with you staying at my place."

I would really enjoy pushing his buttons for a while (he is kinda cute when he's panicking) but I let him off the hook, "Relax, Darren. I'm not about to sofa surf. I'm on the company's dime. I've booked a room at the Marriot."

"On the company dime. Great! So you won't mind springing for happy hour."

We take a quick walk and end up at a place called the 'Over/Under Bar and Grill'. Not wasting any time, Darren catches the eye of the bartender and says "Hey, Becky. Two of the usual. Thanks." He makes his way to a booth that looks well-worn and grabs a seat. I sit opposite and stash my carryon under the table.

"So... out with it. Why St. Louis? Why now? Why me?" He's all questions, and I guess I don't blame him.

"Whoa, slow down there, Darren. I've barely gotten off the plane and you're quizzing me like we're on some sort of game show. Don't I deserve a bit of foreplay before you jump right in like that?"

I can see the use of the word 'foreplay' has had the desired effect. Darren is left speechless as the word gyrates around in that fertile imagination of his. Now that I've gained the upper hand, I can ask questions at my own pace.

"So, remember back in the day when you were a lowly local beat writer instead of the guy who pisses everyone off with your op-ed pieces?" I ask, somewhat tongue in cheek.

"Well, of course I remember those days... since I only started on the editorial desk less than a year ago. And for the record, my memory is stellar and my op-ed pieces don't piss off everyone. Just the illogical readers."

"Well, great to see you haven't lost your sense of self-righteousness. Even better to hear that your memory is intact. I have some questions about a story you may remember, or even have worked on. Do you recall a little girl and a near drowning in Lafayette Park? She was saved by a mystery man? Would have been in September 2007."

"Yup. I remember it well, actually. I did work on it. Why do you ask? That was well over two years ago. I get that the magazine you work for doesn't pay much attention to the news cycles, but even for you guys, that's ancient news."

He can't help the subtle dig. Most of the ink-stained wretches that are still employed by newspapers seem to have a certain arrogance and don't try very hard to hide their disdain for journalists who work outside of that media. It's actually quite bizarre given that their employers are slowly becoming extinct, while digital media and boutique print media are thriving.

I let the dig slide and give him the basics of the story I'm chasing: three little kids, different states, saved from near-death by a mystery man who gives a fake name then disappears. After I've finished, I'm happy to see that I've got his full attention.

"So, you suspect this guy is either a serial killer or some kind of Johnny-on-the-spot baby saver. That's interesting. Maybe there's a follow-up story for the Post-Dispatch in this. All right, I'm willing to help. What specifically do you want from me?"

"Well, first of all... you were there, right? Did anything seem off to you? I mean, this guy, did he seem strange in any way?"

Darren looks slightly deflated. "Well, yes, I was there. But, I wasn't there when he was there. By the time I arrived at the scene he'd vanished."

"Okay. Let's start from the beginning. What did you see, and when?"

He pauses briefly, thinking, then responds. "All right. I'm going on memory here, but I can confirm this later... Basically, I picked up the story when a call came in over the police services line. I arrived at the park right after the cops, paramedics and that talking head from News Channel 7 had arrived. The paramedics checked over the little girl, just to make sure she was okay and not in shock or anything. The mother was taken aside by the police and I managed to catch most of their conversation."

"That's good. That's what I'm looking for. So,

what were they talking about?" I'm feeling somewhat excited by the prospect of getting some first-hand information about the incident.

He continues, "They confirmed that the lady, who I think was named Elvira, or something like that... we can check later... was the little girl's mother. They asked her to describe the events in detail. She cried quite a bit. She felt guilty because she had been distracted by her new phone and the messaging going on with her ex-husband. The cops clued in on this and asked her when she became aware of the man and her daughter. She said she only noticed him when he came to her child's rescue, and that she didn't really know where he'd come from. They then asked her if she thought it was possible that the man had lured her little girl to the pond."

"So, what did she say to that? This is important."

"No shit, Sherlock," he says somewhat testily. "You aren't the only one with a journalism degree. Anyhow, the lady pondered that for a moment, then shook her head and answered very clearly that she didn't think that was possible. She would have noticed something like that. And besides, she said, the man was a hero... not a creep."

I roll this around my mind for a bit. "So, I'm getting the impression that the cops were a bit skeptical. Let's face it, they aren't real fond of men loitering near the kiddies' playground. At any rate, I think I'd like to talk to the cop. You wouldn't happen to have a name, would you?"

"I did have, and even included it in my original story. But the editor wanted to take it in a different direction. The police angle never made it into the story that was published. Instead we focused on the mysterious Good Samaritan. We ran one more short article as a follow up. The kid's mom had raised some money as a reward and was looking to connect with our mystery man Gordon Howe, but she wasn't having any luck. Basically, it was a shout out to our readership to help track him down. It came to nothing. He just vanished into thin air."

"Okay. This is really good, Darren. Do you think you could dig up the officer's info for me, and maybe the name and address of the mom?" I ask, batting my eyelashes and using my blinding smile as shamelessly as I can. He is putty in my hands.

"Sure, I can do that... if you buy us another round and promise to keep me in the loop going forward. If this guy turns out to be a pervert or sociopath, I want in."

"Deal," I say.

We clink glasses, down our Manhattans, and Darren provides Becky with the international sign language for 'another round', twirling his right index finger up in the air. Something tells me Becky has seen his act before, but she hides it well with a smile, and goes about her business. I've seen this before too, so I make a point of telling him, "I have to go after this drink. I have my masters to report to, and I haven't

114

even checked in to my hotel yet. Can you call me tomorrow with those names and addresses?"

He looks slightly disappointed at the abruptness of my pending departure, but nods his head in agreement. I'm off to a good start, and so far the information has come fairly cheaply.

True to his word, Darren calls me early the next morning. "Hey beautiful. Did I wake you up?"

"No, but I just got out of the shower. Can I call you back?"

"Wait. Let me savour that vision for a while. No... no need for you to call me back. This won't take a minute. Check your email."

I grab my phone from the bedside table and scroll through my emails. Sure enough, there's one from Darren's personal email address, BigDickDarren@hotmail.com. The man has no shame. I open the email and quickly scan the content: names and addresses as requested.

"This is great. Thanks Darren, I owe you one."

"Music to my ears. And, you can bet I'll be cashing in on that at some point."

"I'm counting on it. Maybe I can take you and your girlfriend out for dinner sometime." I don't know why I say that. I've never met the woman and I'm not even clear on how serious their relationship is. Perhaps it's a bit of a fishing exhibition. It's second nature in my business, but, if I'm honest with myself, maybe it's more than that.

Darren doesn't miss a beat. "Trust me, if I'm cashing in a favour, it won't be to sit through a dinner with you and Trish. Besides, by the time we get together again, Trish might be gone. To be honest, I'm really not into her all that much."

If I'm fishing, this would be considered a catch. A tidbit of information to file away for future reference. Despite myself, I like hearing this news. After all, NYU was a long time ago. We've managed to stay in touch, and I consider my friendship with Darren strong. Maybe, when I'm ready to settle down... but who knows when that will be.

I gather my wits and sign off, "Well... thanks all the same. I'll be in touch. And Darren... please change your email id." We both have a bit of laugh, then hang up.

I get dressed and wander down to the Marriot restaurant for some coffee and a pastry. Re-reading my email from BigDickDarren, I ponder my next moves. I think the best plan would be to talk to the officer who arrived at the scene (now Captain Dunn of the Fifth Precinct, formerly Sergeant Dunn). He might be able to point me to other witnesses at the scene who were not in the newspaper article but could share some information about Gordon Howe. Time permitting, I could speak with them, then when school is out, head over to the mother and daughter's home (identified in full by Darren's email as Elmira and Flora Brown of 38 Deerfield Crescent).

I dial directory assistance. "Hello, can you

connect me to the St. Louis Police Department Fifth Precinct please?"

"Is this an emergency, ma'am?" After I confirm it is not, she continues, "One moment please, while I connect your call."

"Fifth Precinct, Sergeant Dryden. How can I help you?"

"I'd like to speak with Captain Dunn, please."

There is a pause on the line. Clearly Sergeant Dryden isn't in the habit of directing calls to his captain. "Who may I ask is calling, and what is the nature of your call?"

"My name is Joanne Hope, and I'm an investigative journalist. I'm working on a story and I'd like to speak with your captain about my investigation."

"Well, Ms. Hope, the captain is a very busy man. I'm going to patch you through to our media relations department and you can see what they have to say." And, with that, I find myself within the bureaucracy of the St. Louis Police Department. After several conversations with various handlers, I finally find myself back with Sergeant Dryden.

"Well, Sergeant, that was an interesting tour of police red tape. I'm sure that Captain Dunn will speak with me now that I have the consent of your media handlers."

"We'll see about that. Now, Ms. Hope, let me get your particulars and I will leave a message with Captain Dunn."

I leave the cranky Sergeant Dryden with my

contact information and decide to check out the scene of the incident in Lafayette Park while I'm waiting for his return call (which may or may not come if I'm reading the sergeant right). I grab a cab outside the hotel and in a few minutes find myself overlooking the pond where the toddler Flora was presumably rescued from drowning. It's actually quite lovely and quiet. Hard to picture such a traumatic event happening here. My phone buzzing takes me out of my contemplation. "Joanne Hope," I answer.

"Ms. Hope. This is Captain Dunn with the St. Louise Police Department. You called earlier about an investigation you're working on. My media relations folks checked your credentials and said I should call you back. Seems they are impressed with your work."

I pick up the hint of a chuckle in this last comment. "Well, I'm flattered that they put in a good word for me. I know you are busy, so I won't waste your time. Do you recall about two and a half years ago you worked a case involving a little girl and a near drowning in Lafayette Park?"

"Yes. I do recall that case. Let me pull it up on my laptop so I have a bit more context." A pause, then, "Yes, here it is. Little girl Flora, mother Elmira."

"Yes, that's the one. I'm actually interested in the hero of the story. He gave his name as Gordon Howe, claimed to be from Detroit."

"Well, Ms. Hope, we both know that's not his real name. Right?" He chuckles.

I reply, "Unless a former NHL superstar was

homeless and wandering the streets of St. Louis, I'm pretty sure it's an alias." I laugh. I think Captain Dunn was giving me a little test and I just passed. "So, I take it this alias drew a bit of suspicion?" I ask, hopefully leading him to divulge more.

The captain pauses, and I hear him sigh. Finally he tells his story. "The whole thing seemed off to me. Why did he use an alias and just disappear into thin air? And, trust me, he did disappear. Either his homeless pals didn't want to talk, or they truly had no idea where he was."

He's silent for a moment, so I prompt him, "And, tell me, why were you so interested in finding him? Did you suspect something?"

"Well, in a situation like this, where a child is involved in any kind of life-threatening incident, we have to question everyone involved. He was a loose thread. But that's not all. His disappearance made me think he had something to hide. You can see why I'd be suspicious. The mother, Elmira, insisted that there was nothing shady going on. She said he was a hero. But she can't really vouch for the exact whereabouts of her child just prior to the accident. Was her kid lured? Did this Gordon Howe character do something to the little girl, then try to cover his tracks? But... if that's the case... then why save her? Maybe he couldn't go through with it. We had some of our child psychologists speak with the little girl, Flora, and they seemed to think that the near drowning traumatized her, as expected, but no abuse of any kind happened before that. But, I don't know, it still eats at me. Why the magical disappearing act?"

"Why, indeed? Your impression is much like my own. Well, that's it for now, Captain. Thank you very much for your time."

Just about to hang up, Captain Dunn interrupts. "Wait a minute, Ms. Hope. Don't you think you owe me a bit of an explanation? Why is a Pulitzer nominee interested in an old investigation? Do you want to fill me in?"

I hesitate. I'm not sure what I should share with him at this point. But, he is right. I do owe him something. I owe him a heads up at least. "Well, Captain, all I can tell you at this time is that I'm interested because it appears that this might not have been an isolated incident. And, like you, I want to track down Mr. Howe."

The gravity of what I've just told him hits home. "Oh, I see. So, there's a chance we'll be re-opening this case... is that what you are saying?"

"That's exactly what I'm saying. But, trust me on this, Captain Dunn. You are a busy man and I'm sure you are never anxious to re-open cases. I will run this to ground and, if things don't add up, you will definitely be brought into the loop. We'd be talking multi-state investigation... and you know what that means..." I leave that hanging. The thought of FBI involvement is all I need to hint at.

"Yes, I know what that means. And you know that I know... and you also know that the prospect doesn't much appeal to me. Nevertheless, if it comes to that, I trust you will give me a heads up."

"You know it." And with that, I bid the good captain adieu. I find it is always good practice to ensure law enforcement is on the same page (or, better yet, roughly one page behind) when I'm running down a story. You want them on your side, but on your terms. Mission accomplished, and without me having to resort to my feminine wiles. That's rare where law enforcement is concerned.

I get to the Brown household around 4:30 p.m. Early enough that school is out, but not so late that I'd interrupt dinner time preparations. It's a modest home in a nice neat middle class neighborhood. Close to the park where the incident occurred, I can see where raising children here would have immense appeal. As I approach the veranda that runs the width of the house I can hear a child's laughter coming from inside. It's times like this that my biological clock reminds me that my time for having children is rapidly running out. At 42, some would say it's already run out, but, I'm blessed with my mother's genes and she didn't hit menopause until she was 56. She likes to remind me of that every time I see her.

Anyhow, after pushing these thoughts deep down into the psychological abyss where I store all my desires and anxieties, I ring the doorbell. I hear more fits of laughter as the door flies open, and, there before me I see a very animated little girl about five old. Her laughter stops, and her big brown eyes widen. "Mommy! There's a stranger at the door!"

She promptly runs from the entrance, and a woman comes hustling into the entry way, gently scolding her. "Flora, you know you shouldn't open the door to anyone without knowing who they are, but I'm glad you knew this was a stranger and you came to get me right away."

The whole scene unfolds so quickly, yet so poignantly, that I'm temporarily at a loss for words. Thankfully I quickly recover and introduce myself. "Hello, Ms. Brown? My name is Joanne Hope," I say, showing her my business card as she nods. "I'm an investigative reporter for the magazine 'Atlantic Quarterly'. I'm sorry to come unannounced like this, but I'm on a pretty tight schedule and was in the neighborhood... so... here I am. Would you mind sparing a few minutes to talk to me?"

Elmira, wearing an apron over a modest print dress, eyes me suspiciously while I'm tap dancing on her front porch. Arms crossed, she doesn't look at all inviting. Then, I see her facial expression change. "Wait, Joanne Hope. I've heard of you. You wrote that article and helped nab those scum bags who ran that prostitution ring in Fargo, right?" I nod, and she continues, "Well sure, why don't you come on in? I'll make some tea and we can have a nice chat." We shake hands and she practically drags me over the threshold and into her living room. "Please, have a seat. I'll be right back."

She hustles out of the room, leaving me with her little girl, who is now perched on a small stool watching cartoons on low volume, but who also seems very interested in the strange lady that mommy is suddenly fussing over. Her curiosity gets the better of her shyness.

"My name is Flora, what's your name?"

"My name is Joanne."

"That's a nice name, Joanne, I like that. I'm five, how old are you?"

"I'm forty-two."

"Is that old?"

"I don't think so."

"I don't think so either, you don't look old." Oh, from the mouths of babes. She is adorable.

Elmira returns carrying a tray with a tea pot, two mugs, and a few cookies that catch Flora's attention.

"Ms. Brown... thank you. You didn't have to go to all this trouble, and I really don't want to take too much of your time."

"No trouble at all. And you can call me Elmira."

"Okay, Elmira. Please call me Joanne."

Ice broken, I get right to the point. "So, Elmira, I have some questions about Flora's near drowning incident two years ago. Are we okay to discuss that?"

"Why, sure, we are okay to discuss that. Did you find Mr. Howe?"

I'm surprised by her question, but also think it interesting that she still seems concerned about his whereabouts. "No, he has not been found, although I'm working on that. What I want to ask you is if you could describe to me what occurred that day."

"Okay. My memory is still very clear on the day – it was the scariest day of my life. Flora was almost three, and I was really enjoying that time with her because she was really becoming a little person, you know? She was always talking and asking questions and running around poking her nose into things. A real handful... but in a good way. I loved explaining things to her and watching her mind turn things over. Still do, actually. Anyway, we went to the park just about every day back then. That day it was sweltering hot and we decided to go to the kiddie pool so she could splash around. I was a bit pre-occupied because I was texting back and forth with her good-for-nothing father about child support. You know, that man, he still owes me several months of back payments. Anyway, like I said, I was on my phone, and I'm ashamed to admit it, I wasn't paying enough attention to Flora. She was a bit fussy, maybe because of the heat, then she stopped crying and seemed content to splash about in the shallow kids' pool. Next thing I know, I look up from my phone and she's gone. I panic and start running around looking for her. I make a beeline towards the pond, because she was always curious about it, and I'm terrified she might have wandered over there. Sure enough, there she was... face down in the water..."

She pauses to catch her breath and wipe a tear from the corner of her eye. "Sorry... I still get upset just thinking about it. I was in hysterics. I don't even know what I was yelling, but then out of nowhere this man appears. He pulled off his hiking boots and backpack, and he's running towards the pond. He plunges in and he looks like that Mark Spitz from the Olympics back in the day. I've never seen a man swim so fast. He gets to Flora and flips her over and gets her back to the shoreline in no time. He starts giving her CPR. Meanwhile, a bunch of people who must have heard me carrying on had gathered around. They all start pulling out their phones, taking pictures and whatnot. At that time, I could care less, but now when I think about it, it kind of bothers me that they were doing that. Anyway, I was too busy watching Mr. Howe with Flora. After a few pumps to the chest and some mouth to mouth, Flora coughs up a lung full of water and starts sputtering and coughing. I was overwhelmed! She was breathing, and she starts calling 'Mommy! Mommy!' I take her in my arms and tell her that she's all right, that this nice man saved her. She looks at him and has the funniest look on her face. Almost like she's hypnotized. Then she smiles the biggest brightest smile. My heart just expanded at the sight of it. I still get goosebumps thinking of that smile."

"And what was Mr. Howe doing at this point?" I ask.

"Well I thank him, and he's kind of modest and nice. Other people start slapping him on the back and shaking his hand. Then this one guy, who I'd seen in the park before... I think he's homeless... he comes up to him and they shake hands and the guy says something to him I couldn't hear, then they beeline it out of there. Mr. Howe takes one look back, waves to Flora and she waves back... and that's the last we've ever seen of him. Then some paramedics and police arrive .... And some news folks from channel seven. It took us another hour to get out of there. The police had all kinds of questions, but I guess they must have been okay with what happened because I never heard from them again. Some guy with a cell phone showed us a video that he took and asked us if we minded if he shared it. I told him I didn't care what he did with it. I was a little rude to him. Later that night Flora and I watched the news together. She was so happy to see us both on the TV."

"Did the police ask you many questions about Mr. Howe?" I questioned.

"Oh sure. They asked me if I knew him, if I'd ever seen him in the park before. All I could tell them was his name, Gordon Howe, and that he told me he was from Detroit. That's all I really knew about him, other than he could swim like an Olympian. I think the police took down the names and contact information of the witnesses too, and later checked their cell phone videos."

I was curious what her thinking was about the police inquiries. "Why do you think they were so interested in Mr. Howe?"

"Well, they didn't come out and say it, but I think they suspected he might be a pervert or something, and that maybe he lured Flora into that water. If they had asked me, I'd have told them they were nuts. My Flora, we call her 'Flora the Explora', she didn't need to be lured anywhere. She'd be off on her own the minute I turned my head. I learned my lesson that day. God had mercy on me that day. I have never had let her out of my sight again, that's for sure. And, besides, if they had seen the way Mr. Howe and Flora looked and smiled at each other.... there was no way that man would ever hurt her or any other child."

I wrap it up quickly with Elmira. I promise her that if I track down Mr. Howe I will let her know how to get in touch with him. As I'm preparing to leave, Flora gives me an unsolicited hug and a formal "It was nice to meet you, Joanne," mimicking her mother. My stomach (and/or uterus) is groaning. It's time to have some lunch then try to track down the homeless man in the park to see what light he might be able to shed on our mysterious Mr. Howe.

Back at the hotel, I change into my jeans, fleece, windbreaker, plaid shirt and hiking boots. I take the backpack I'd packed away in my carryon, stash a hotel towel in it with my small handbag, and head down to the lobby, where they have conveniently placed a wine store. I purchase a cheap bottle of red wine and stick it in my backpack. After grabbing a quick lunch at the hotel restaurant, I head on foot to Lafayette Park. It's a bit chilly, and that seems to have kept traffic in the park to a minimum. It doesn't take me long to locate the kiddie pool and the pond, which in my opinion are dangerously close to each other. After scouring the area for a while and getting a sense of what might have happened back in September 2007, I widen my search in hopes of tracking down the man who Elmira said frequents the park, and appeared to know our mystery man.

Not far from the public washrooms near the kiddie pool, I spy a man in a sleeping bag sprawled out on a park bench. Under the bench I spot a couple of empty liquor bottles. This could be our man. I decide the best way to approach him is to play the role of a drifter myself, at least until I gain his trust. With that in mind, I spread my hotel towel behind the bench, and start rummaging underneath it to gather his empties. This has the intended consequences.

"Hey. what are you doing there, lady?"

"Oh, sorry. Didn't mean to wake you. Just collecting empties. I need to scrape together some bus fare."

"Well, normally I'd say bugger off. But you are at least polite, and honest about it. Be my guest."

Now that I've broken the ice, I can push my advantage. "Thank you, that's nice of you. It's not often people are nice to people like me."

He slowly emerges from his sleeping bag, looks me over with a blurry eye and asks, "Are you on the streets? You don't look it."

"No, I'm not exactly homeless. I'm just your basic restless soul, backpacking around, exploring. Name's Joanne. I've got a home back in Philly with my parents, but I needed an adventure. What about you?"

"Well, I'm Joey, and as my friend the Professor used to say, I'm an urban camper." With that he chuckles. And with that I also latch onto discussion of his friend, who sounds like he's not around any longer.

"That's a good one. Urban camper. Say, how about a little afternoon snort, Joey?" I pull out my wine bottle and watch his eyes widen. I twist off the cap, take a swig and offer it to him. "Least I can do since you're kind enough to donate your empties."

"Don't mind if I do." He takes the bottle and has a long pull from it.

I try to keep the conversation going. "So, tell me about this 'Professor' friend of yours. He sounds like quite the character."

"Oh, he was. He was an urban camper himself, but you'd not know to look at him right off. He was always pretty well groomed and carried himself with a certain confidence. Seemed pretty smart, educated. The only time you'd know he wasn't part of mainstream society is when he got really drunk, which was pretty much every evening, then he'd be like the rest of us. He had demons. They'd come out."

"Oh, I get that. We all carry baggage. What happened to him?"

"Interesting story, that. One September morning a couple of years back I was here sleeping it off – not really all together myself – when I hear this ruckus over by the pond, a lady yelling for help. It gets my attention and I get over there just in time to see the

Professor swimming like Tarzan of the jungle towards this little girl who's face down in the pond. He ends up giving her CPR and saving her life. The mother goes from being hysterical to crying tears of joy. It really was something to see. Anyhow, after the ruckus, I didn't have anything to drink, and by then, by God, we both needed something. So we head to the bus station just a couple blocks from here. A lot of our fellow campers hang out there and we figure we can scrounge off them 'til we can purchase our own. When we get there, it's like a hero's welcome for the Professor. He's up on the TV screen and all the crew is watching. There's a few toasts, then, just as things are settling down, he vanishes. I didn't even get a chance to say goodbye."

Bingo.

He pauses in his story-telling. "So, do you know where the Professor went?" I prompt.

"I asked around. One of the guys said he saw him hop on a bus heading for Nashville. I guess maybe he didn't like being a celebrity. And, I can't say I blame him. When you live your life being invisible like most of us urban campers do, you usually don't like the glare of the spotlight."

As we share some more wine, Joey starts to tell me a bit about himself. I deftly turn the conversation back to the Professor. "So, Joey, was this man actually a professor? Did he ever mention where he was from?"

"I don't know for sure if he actually was a professor, but I don't think he was. He just naturally got that nickname 'cause he was pretty well-spoken and he read some good books. He hung around this park for around two years. I don't remember him saying where he was from, but when he was drunk he'd sometimes talk about Detroit. He'd rant about the Detroit police, the Detroit highways, the Detroit sports teams. There seemed to be a connection. Then we all got a good laugh when that reporter on TV referred to him as Gordon Howe."

I let Joey finish the bottle and start to make my move to leave. "Well, Joey, it's been nice chatting with you."

"My pleasure, Miss Joanne. Now, don't forget those empties. Every little bit helps. Oh, to be young again and seeing the country like you're doing."

Then, for some reason I can't explain, I tell him the truth. "Joey, I'm going to let you keep those empties and get that refund yourself. The truth is, I'm not a backpacker roaming the country. I'm a reporter. And I want you to know, you've helped me. I'm looking for your man, who you call the Professor. I think his story is interesting, and I plan on writing that story."

Joey looks a bit confused. Then he just shakes his head. "Well, I'm sure his story is interesting. And, for the record, I never bought your backpacker story one hundred percent. Just tell me one thing. Is the Professor in trouble?"

"Truthfully, I don't know. I don't think so. But I plan to find out."

Joey ponders that, then says with certainty, "Well, if he is in trouble, it's all a misunderstanding. The

Professor was the straightest arrow I've ever known. You can quote me in your story."

    We part ways with a handshake. Joey has confirmed that the man who saved Flora in St. Louis hopped a bus for Nashville and it seems more than likely it was him who ended up saving another youngster. More importantly, Joey filled in a blank for me. It looks like our story might have started in Detroit.

Jacksonville, January 2010

My latest brush with unwanted celebrity in Atlanta has shaken me badly. They say two times is a coincidence, but three times is a pattern. Well, I don't like this pattern. Not one bit. I chose to remain anonymous for a reason. Being part of the news landscape on a regular basis is not at all what I want. What I really want is to slide into a drunk coma and never awaken again.

I take stock of my situation. The truth is, I've been negligent. My goal to drink myself into an early grave is far behind schedule. I chastise myself for my lack of commitment, but I'm also buoyed by the fact that my foray into self-employment in Atlanta replenished my rainy day fund beyond my wildest dreams. I think – and hope – Jacksonville will be my last stop. I can afford to drink all day every day and, with any luck, slide into the big sleep I so desperately now seek and desire.

Fueling this desire is the endless loop I keep playing in my head. First the toddler in St. Louis, then the baby in Nashville, then little Emmaline in Atlanta. I don't doubt for a second that I'd do it all over again, but I can't stop the cacophony in my head that keeps screaming "Why? Why me? Why?" Of course, I know one way to stop it. And to stop it for good. Drink. I need to drink and I need to keep drinking.

Since arriving in Jacksonville, that has been precisely what I have been doing. I've not found a place where I regularly sleep, nor do I care. I sometimes find myself under the Interstate 95 bridge where it bisects the St. John River, usually in the undergrowth by the river. Just east of the bridge, a couple of blocks from the river bank, there is a store where I buy most of my liquor... Big Al's. I buy booze when I wake up, and drink until I pass out. I've ceased caring about my appearance. No more washing, brushing hair, brushing teeth. The clothes I'm wearing are the same ones I arrived in... which I think might have been a month ago, although I have no real sense of time anymore. Still, the second I regain any sense of coherent thought, there are only two things that come to mind: "Why is this happening to me?" Followed closely by, "Who cares? Get drunk." Which I do. Rinse, repeat. The days and nights all seem numbingly the same. Which suits me fine. I don't need any more drama in my life. I need to really just slide into oblivion. Another unknown soul – dead of exposure, liver failure, or any number of violent crimes.

It has not gone unnoticed by my fellow urban campers that I seem to have a stash of cash somewhere. Twice in the last couple of weeks I've taken a beating. But I'm smart enough not to keep all of my worldly possessions with me, including my stash. My assailants are sharp enough to not work me over too hard, since they quickly discover that I don't keep much on me and also, since I often share my purchases, if they kill me it would be much like killing the goose who laid the golden egg. Too bad I can't run into someone violent enough and stupid enough to finish the job.

I've also contemplated 'death by cop'. Once, when I was very intoxicated, the fat bastard at Big Al's refused to sell me any more alcohol. The likelihood of being shot by the cashier or the responding police officers should I decide to become violent and make a feeble attempt at robbery, briefly appealed to me. But then the old cowardice that has plagued me now for years took over. Instead, I staggered down the street a few blocks and bought beer from a place that is much less stringent about who they do business with. I made it a point of going back to Big Al's and displaying my purchase to fat boy. The message was clear. Sell me alcohol or someone else will. I've never had a problem with him since. I'm certain by the scowl on his face every time I enter the place that he despises me, but he's not about to let that interfere with our business relationship. Sometimes I'm too smart for my own good (or too cowardly). My survival instinct keeps me from a confrontation that might do what I'm too afraid to do myself.

Now, as I sit in the mud near the river, cradling my jug of Jack Daniel's, I can feel some satisfaction. I don't recall the last solid meal I ate. Also, I'm starting to have all the common tell-tale signs of liver failure. My eyes and skin have taken on a distinctive yellowing color, according to the more honest of my fellow urban campers. My previously taut mid-section is starting to swell. And in the mornings (or whenever I wake) I'm often confused, with my arms and legs swollen and aching. So, I feel my goal is within reach. I drink heavily from my bottle of Jack, then swear softly to myself. "Fuck this useless life. And fuck the powers that be and all their fucking evil little games. Fuck you for fucking me. Fuck you for fucking up everything and fuck me for giving a fuck."

With any luck, I'll be dead by Easter.

January 2010, St. Louis to Nashville

I check in with Tony, filling him in on what I'd found out so far. He almost seemed disappointed that, so far, our mystery man, who I now call 'the Professor', doesn't appear to be a serial child killer.

"So, what you're telling me is, we have some random guy, presumably from Detroit, who just stumbles into situations and saves the day," Tony drones over the phone.

"But, there's more to it, Tony. This guy has a back story. By all accounts, he so far sounds like he was a good citizen who went off the rails for some reason, became homeless and a drunk. And then these things start to happen. I'm telling you, there is something there, and the only way to find out what that 'something' is, is to find the Professor. He's the story."

"So you keep saying. But what I don't get is, if you think he's from Detroit, why not go there? Why Nashville?"

"Because we won't find him in Detroit, and so far I have no information about him in Detroit. I have to follow the trail forward and hopefully find him. Then we can ask about Detroit and other places he might have lived or visited."

"All right, we can rule out Detroit for now. But what about Atlanta? Why not pick up the trail there?"

I knew this question would come, as I had debated that very question with myself. I explain my rationale to Tony. "There are two reasons. First, the stories in Nashville versus Atlanta are very different. Nashville has a lot of holes, so there's more to find out. The overdosed young woman and her child were never named in the news story, whereas we know the names of the events in Atlanta but we don't know if they are directly connected to the Professor. I want to find out if there is a possible family connection in Nashville. Second, I need to get more details for the story I'm writing. It just makes sense to go there and follow the chronology. I'll go to Atlanta on my next stop, after I get a better picture of what went down in Nashville."

There is silence on the other end, followed by a heavy sigh. "Okay, I suppose you're right. That said, what are your chances of meeting our deadline? Randal's going to want to know."

I pause, mainly for effect. "Well, I called Jerome before I called you. He still wants me to see this through and he doesn't really care how I approach it. But, in answer to your question, you know that I will do all that I can to make that deadline."

"Good." And with that an abrupt end to our call. Tony hates it when I do an end around, but I just can't help myself.

I don't bother stopping at home. I have everything I need. I opt to go directly from St. Louis to Nashville via Southwest. It's a non-stop flight and I'm in the air for about an hour and a half, but by the time I add in all the airport time and travel between hotels and airports, it's closer to a four hour trip.

On the flight I'd refreshed my memory by re-

reading the Nashville article about the young mother who overdosed and her son who was rescued from a hot car. It looks like the action all took place fairly close to the tourist district, so on landing I consult a map of the city and decide on the Hyatt House as my base of operations.

Arriving at the downtown Hyatt House, I'm too bushed to do anything other than wash my underthings and tee shirt in the sink, and pass out naked on the bed. I awaken around 8 p.m., throw on some jeans along with my white silk shirt, which is usually reserved for my power suit. I untangle the knots from my hair, don my heels and make my way to the lobby, where I find the hotel bar. After ordering a Manhattan, I review the menu and order some smoked ribs and a garden salad. I nibble at my food, my mind preoccupied with my next moves. I have two people I need to start with: the bus driver who was interviewed about the events, and the police officer who investigated. The bus driver should be pretty easy to track down... his name was mentioned in the article as Sid Ferraro. I can phone the tour operators and get a line on him. The police are a different story. There was no named officer, just a contact number to call if anyone had further information. Maybe it's time to give my friendly cop back in St. Louis a call and see if he can grease the wheels for me.

After a good night's sleep, slightly aided by the two Manhattans I had with dinner, I'm raring to go. But I need not go far to start. My plan is to work the phone this morning, then head out to track down any leads. My first calls are to the various tour operators that advertise gambling junkets. After dealing with a receptionist, I generally get transferred to a human resources person. I need to tread carefully here, as sometimes companies are not too forthcoming about their employees. I call this 'dead-beat dad syndrome'. It amazes me how some people who owe child support can hide behind their employers.

"Hello. My name is Joanne Hope. I'm an investigative reporter for the 'Atlantic Quarterly', doing a follow up piece on an incident that one of your employees might have been witness to. Do you by chance employ a driver by the name of Sid Ferraro?"

I hit 'pay dirt', as the gamblers say, on my third call.

"Can you be more specific as to the nature of the incident?" I've anticipated this question. The last thing a tour operator probably wants to be involved in is being a party to a traffic accident, even as a witness. Regardless of their involvement, they shy away from that specific type of inquiry.

"Sure. Last August Mr. Ferraro was witness to a baby boy being rescued from an overheated car by a man who went by the name of Brett Hull, who then went missing. Mr. Ferraro was quoted in a newspaper article about the incident and I'm just trying to track him down to ask some follow-up questions."

"Oh, I see. Of course I remember it. Sid was quite shaken by the whole thing. Tell you what, Ms.

Hope, if you leave your contact information I will pass it along through our dispatch center. If he is willing to speak with you, he will call you back."

I leave my phone number, the best I can do for now. I thank the HR rep and move onto my next call.

After running the gauntlet of police red tape at the St. Louis Fifth Precinct, I'm finally connected with Captain Dunn. "Well, Ms. Hope, I didn't expect to hear from you again so quickly. What can I do for you? Or, better yet, what can you do for me?"

"Perhaps it's a quid pro quo situation, Captain. I'll go first. I've got a lead on your mystery man, the guy who was involved in the baby saver incident that we recently discussed. He hopped a bus from St. Louis and ended up in Nashville. He has another alias, 'the Professor'."

A pause, then the captain responds, "That's interesting, I suppose. Where did you get this information?"

"I spoke with a homeless man in St. Louis who knew the Professor, and followed the lead. I'm in Nashville now, which is where I come to the quid pro quo part. Do you happen to have any contacts on the Nashville force?"

"Not so fast. Why would Nashville police be interested in this man?"

This is the sticky part. I don't want Captain Dunn to get too excited about what I know, but I can't keep him totally in the dark. "Well, without getting into too much detail, there's been a similar incident here in

Nashville. I'm trying to connect the dots and need some assistance from Nashville's finest. That's where you come in. Can you help grease the wheels or not?"

"Ms. Hope, why do I get the feeling I'm being played? You realize of course, that if we have someone of suspicion in two incidents like this that cross state lines we may have to bring in the Feds. And I think I've made myself pretty clear on how I feel about that."

"Yes, you've made that perfectly clear. That said, I've no evidence of any wrong doing. And, I promise you, if there is any potential for FBI involvement, it will be you who calls them in. Not Nashville. As I told you before, you get the heads-up first."

"Okay, I think we have an understanding. Let me make a couple of calls and I'll get back to you. I still have your contact info. I'll be in touch." He hangs up abruptly and I'm left wondering if I've finessed this the right way or if he's just paying lip service at this point.

I order room service for breakfast and wait patiently for my cell phone to ring. It doesn't take long. I quickly wash back the toast I'm chewing with some coffee and answer anxiously, "Joanne Hope."

"Hi, Ms. Hope. This is Sid Ferraro. I got a call from our HR rep and they told me you wanted to talk to me about that young woman who overdosed last year, and her poor baby."

I'm thrilled to hear back from him so soon. "Thanks very much for calling me, Mr. Ferraro. Yes, I do want to talk with you about that incident. I'd prefer to meet you in person to discuss it though, is that possible sometime today?"

"Sure. I did an overnight from Memphis, so I have today off. But I'd like to avoid rush hours if possible."

"How about the Marriot downtown, at noon? Meet me in the lobby then I'll buy you some lunch and a beer?"

"Ms. Hope, I like your style. I'll see you there."

Nothing like feeding a person to get them to open up. And besides, that will be an hour more for me to be on the job this afternoon instead of sitting around waiting. I finish up my breakfast and have a perfunctory shower. It's barely ten a.m. and I'm starting to feel restless. This is how these things go. It's not linear. You make some quick progress, then stall for a bit. I have to be patient, or I will go a bit crazy.

I spend some time on the AP wire (after all, I always need to be sniffing for my next story), when my phone rings again. I'm hoping that it's Captain Dunn or some other police official, and I'm not disappointed. I pick up quickly. "Hello?"

"Hello. Is this Joanne Hope?"

"Yes, this is she. Whom may I ask is calling?" I love the formal greeting. It tends to knock people off balance.

"This is Captain John Marvel from the Nashville Police Department. I was contacted by my colleague in the St. Louis PD, Captain Dunn. He brought me up to speed, and tweaked my interest in the story you're working on." I stifle my laughter at his moniker, Captain Marvel. Seems I'm speaking with a super hero.

"Oh, excellent, Captain Marvel." I almost giggle. "I was hoping to hear soon from someone from your PD. I won't rehash what Captain Dunn told you. Do you think you can help me dig a little deeper into what happened? ... Fill me in on what your department knows, or doesn't know, about our homeless hero and his role in the incident?"

"I sure can. But I'd prefer to not do this over the phone. Can you come by the precinct? Say around 2 p.m. today? I'm on the third floor at 200 James Robertson Parkway building, not too far from downtown." I'm feeling almost giddy... another hit for me. "Sure, that's perfect. See you then." I don my silk blouse and power suit, do my makeup, and prepare to head out.

As per our discussion, I meet Sid Ferarro in the hotel lobby at noon and we make our way to the restaurant. He looks to be mid-forties, a bit on the heavy side. He makes no attempt to hide the fact that he is checking me out as we move through the lobby and into the restaurant, but this doesn't bother me; maybe I can use it to my advantage.

We get settled in to a booth, and the waiter comes directly. I feel like it's important for me to take control. "Mr. Ferraro, do you know what you'd like, or do you need a few minutes?"

"Sure... I'll have a Sam Adams and a B.L.T. on

144

whole wheat."

"I'll have a Bloody Mary and a tuna melt.
Thanks. "

"Ms. Hope, please call me Sid. I sure hope I can
help you with your story." He looks into my eyes with a
shy smile, and I wonder if he's contemplating hitting on
me.

"Okay, Sid, and I'm Joanne."

The menu selection and pleasantries taken care
of, I get right down to business. "So, Sid, I read the
newspaper article about the incident that happened last
August, but that's about all I know. Just to confirm, is
this the man you saw that day, who saved that little
boy?" I hold up a picture that I got from a screen
capture of the St. Louis television news reel. It's the
least grainy one I have; not great in terms of quality.

"Yeah, that's him. He was a bit more disheveled
that day in the parking lot, but it was a real steamy day
and he'd just been smashing out a car window."

"So it said in the article that you had left the
scene to find a pay phone, then came back to find the
child rescued... is that right?"

"Yes, that's right. A lot of the bus passengers
were congratulating him, and a couple of the ladies
were calming the baby down. I gathered from someone
in the crowd that he used the handle of his Swiss army
knife in his fist to break through the car window."

"Right. Let's back up a bit. Do you have any
idea where he came from, our Good Samaritan? I
mean... was he already in the lot when you first got

there, or did he come from somewhere else?"

"The lot was pretty empty when I first got there, other than that poor girl's car and some of the tourists that had shown up a bit early. So, no, I didn't notice him when I left for the pay phone. And, he couldn't have come from the north... I would have spotted him. I was trying to find someone who might have a cell phone to call 911."

"Okay. And when you talked to him after... did he give any clue as to why he was there, where he was going... or any indication that he might have known the girl who overdosed?"

"None whatsoever to all those questions. He just confirmed, a bit sheepishly it seemed to me, that he'd broken the window. When I asked him his name, he said he was Brett Hull from St. Louis... which makes me laugh a bit now, because I know who Brett Hull is and I'm pretty sure he isn't this homeless guy."

"Hmm. So, not much to go on. But one more thing. Did he look like a user himself? Any track marks? Did he look high or strung out?"

"No, I don't think he was the type to use a syringe. He was just a boozer. I could smell it on him from a mile away. My guess is he was hanging with the lowlifes that are in the park near the Cumberland River. There might be a few addicts in that crowd, but mostly it's just drunks. But... here's the thing. He might have smelled like a drunk, but he wasn't nasty like some of them. His clothes were relatively clean, he'd shaved recently, his teeth were all there and clean. Just his eyes were blood shot, otherwise if you didn't get a whiff of him you'd just think he was another backpacker visiting Nashville. We get a lot of them. Sometimes they have guitars, playing on the streets for change and hoping for their big break."

"Well, thanks Sid. This helps a bit. I'm getting a better picture of who we're dealing with here." I consider offering him another beer, to be polite, but I'd like to finish this interview and get going so I catch the server's eye and motion for the check.

"I really wish I could tell you more, Joanne. I don't think what I've given you is worth a lunch, but I've enjoyed it just the same," he says with his sweet shy smile.

"Sure it's worth it, Sid. Besides, this goes on the company card." With that, we clink glasses, drink up, and call it a meeting. As we exit the restaurant Sid makes more small talk and ogles my cleavage some more, then reluctantly leaves, wishing me good luck with my story.

I have about twenty minutes to freshen up before I go to the precinct and meet my super hero cop, Captain Marvel. I decide to change into my pencil skirt for this meeting. A gal can never look too good when dealing with law enforcement.

I arrive at the precinct early, which is good, because the desk sergeant isn't in any particular hurry to grant me access to the captain. After he's got a good eyeful of me in my power outfit, lingering on the legs, he asks me the usual questions (name please... what's your business here... do you have an appointment?), then places a call, and a few minutes later he introduces me to Captain Marvel. The captain is a heavy set man, about six feet tall, white, with a carefully manicured salt and pepper beard to match his salt and pepper close cropped hair. As I'm eyeing him, he's sizing me up too, and somewhat disconcertingly, he doesn't seem the least bit impressed.

"Thanks for taking the time," I address the captain as we make our way to the elevator and he punches number three.

"No worries. I'm pleased to meet you. Needless to say, I share Captain Dunn's concerns in this matter."

As we exit the elevator I'm a bit surprised to see that the third floor is homicide division. I wonder, did they treat that girl's overdose as a homicide? Captain Marvel leads me into his office and shuts the door for privacy. An auspicious start.

Following up on the captain's statement, I ask, "You mentioned concerns, Captain. What concerns might those be?"

"Now, Ms. Hope, we all know you're smarter than that. I'll level with you if you level with me, okay? Like Captain Dunn, we have a loose thread in our case. We never got a chance to talk with our 'Mr. Hull', alias 'Mr. Howe', alias 'the Professor'... this newest alias we now know because of you. Typically, we don't spend much time on junkies who overdose. But we're

148

interested in this one for two reasons. First, her overdose was not isolated. There have been a surge of heroin OD's in the past year and we've traced them back to the same supply, which was laced with some really nasty stuff. Second, the grandparents of that baby boy happen to be some pretty important people in this town, and they want some answers."

Suddenly, I feel like I'm the one on the hot seat here, and it's not a feeling I much care for. Time to turn the tables a bit. "So Captain Dunn told you about St. Louis. Did he also tell you that as far as the mother and child in St. Louis believe, our man is a saint?"

"Yes, he mentioned that. But, you and I both know things are not always black and white."

"True", I admit, then continue, "I'm sure you talked to the bus driver, Sid Ferraro. He was pretty convinced that our Good Samaritan wasn't a junky, and that he just happened on the scene. There doesn't seem to be any connection between him and the victim, or heroin for that matter."

"Of course, Mr. Ferraro was the first person we talked to. But you're jumping the gun on your other assumptions. Our tip line yielded a few other lines of investigation." He pauses.

This dance is getting interesting. "Care to enlighten me?"

"Sure. But we need to make a deal first. You know the arrangement you have with Captain Dunn? Well, I want the same. Nobody goes to the Feds without first talking to me and to him. Are we clear on that, Ms. Hope?"

"Crystal clear. Now, fill me in. Why do you think our guy might be a bit suspicious?"

"Well, we found out he'd been in town for roughly two years and was making some under-the-table money at a place called Martin's Bar-B-Q. From there, we talked to a few of his associates. I agree with you he wasn't a junkie. But, with a bit of cash at his disposal and a few connections in Cumberland Park that are known to deal, he could have been in the trade. You don't need a lot of cash to get started in that business. Add that to the fact that a couple of local musicians who he used to associate with have recently been admitted to rehab, and you have a guy who is surrounded by quite a few users. Then, puff... like magic... he disappears right when bodies start to turn up, who are filled with some really toxic shit. And add that to your incident in St. Louis, and we could be dealing with some kind of sociopath. We've got nothing solid, mind you. But, like Captain Dunn, I really want to talk to this guy."

"But, the MO in St. Louis isn't anything like what you are describing. He saved a little girl from drowning. And, there is no indication whatsoever that he was involved in drugs there."

"Yeah. The baby-saver part doesn't quite add up. But, guess what. We matched tox screens with a couple of bodies that turned up in St. Louis right around the time our friend was known to be there. Same batch of nasty shit; same results. Overdoses."

"So, what you are saying is we now have two separate incidents – 'coincidences' – that look suspiciously like they are not coincidences. We have a couple of saved toddlers and a trail of dead junkies that both point to one common denominator: our mysterious Professor."

"That is exactly what I'm saying. Now, Ms. Hope... I've told you all I know. As did Captain Dunn, I believe. Is there anything you aren't sharing with us? Oh, and by the way, at this point you are on record. Now is the time to come clean."

He's making me uncomfortable, which I'm really not used to with law enforcement, especially when I'm wearing my pencil skirt. Then I spot it. There's a desk photo of our Captain with someone who – given their loving smiles – appears to be his life partner. Another man, roughly the same height and age, but of slender build. So no feminine wiles will help me in this situation. Time to spill the beans.

"Okay. I have two things to share with you and Captain Dunn. First, I have reason to believe the Professor traveled to St. Louis from Detroit. I gleaned this from a homeless guy who hangs out in Lafayette Park, where the Professor saved that toddler from drowning. And second... there is one more child who's been saved recently that I think may be tied to the Professor. A youngster in Atlanta was saved after ingesting a toxic substance just this month by a homeless guy who then disappeared. He called himself 'David Legwand'."

"Why do you think it's related to our guy?" he asks.

"You aren't a hockey fan are you, Captain?"

"No. I'm more of a Broadway show guy. So, what's the connection?"

This last bit of personal information that Marvel shares with me appears true to stereotype, and helps confirm my suspicion that he's likely gay. I'm happy to have that confirmed – I thought I was losing my touch.

"Gordon Howe of Detroit, Brett Hull of St. Louis, and David Legwand of Nashville are all former NHL hockey stars... Howe and Hull are Hall of Famers in fact. This is no coincidence. Our Professor is a hockey fan and under pressure he uses hockey player aliases, right before he skips town."

I can see this bombshell has had an effect. Marvel gets up from his desk, paces the room. His mind is churning things over, thinking of his possible options. Finally, after what seems like hours but is in reality is likely only about twenty seconds, he stops, places his hands behind his back and addresses me slowly, in a conspiratorial way.

"All right, here's how we are going to play this, and I'll confirm this with Captain Dunn. Officially, I'm going to re-open the case here in Nashville and file a missing person's report for our Professor. For now, I won't make any reference that this may be a potential child abuse case. Dunn will do the same in St. Louis after I fill him in, I'm sure of it. But, we won't go to the Feds with this just yet. We need to look at what happened in Atlanta, and hopefully get a line on the Professor's whereabouts. If the case in Atlanta fits, and Atlanta PD is onside, we'll all discuss calling in the Feds for assistance in the missing person cases. Any possibility that our guy is a pervert or worse... well, we keep that as close to the vest as possible for now."

I'm not being asked, I'm being told. But in reality, I don't have any cards to play here. My one ray of hope is that like his pal Dunn, Marvel will connect me with Atlanta police and I can do some leg work there before sharing the bigger picture with them. The bigger this thing gets, the more at risk my exclusive rights to the story become.

"Okay, Captain. It sounds like we have an understanding, but, just to be clear, let me paraphrase and interpret what you've said. After I leave here, with full knowledge by the St. Louis and Nashville police departments, you are going to allow me to investigate this third case of heroism in Atlanta by our mystery man. Can I assume you or Captain Dunn will help pave the way with Atlanta PD when I need it?"

"Yes, but we would appreciate you doing some leg work down there first. Check back with us before we bring Atlanta PD into the broader picture, because at that point, depending on what you and they find, we may have no choice but to go to the Feds."

"Okay, that sounds reasonable. But one more thing. Obviously you and Captain Dunn, and soon others I would venture, will all want to have a discussion with the Professor wherever and whenever he turns up. I can promise you that if I find him, you will get that opportunity. Can you promise me the same thing? I want access to him before the Feds do. They have a tendency to make people go silent, and none of us wants that, especially me."

"I think we have a deal, Ms. Hope. I can't promise he won't lawyer up before you get to him, but I can keep the Feds at bay indefinitely... they don't come in until we call them in. And, you can rest assured, Atlanta PD will want it that way too."

"Good. All right... next time I talk with you, I'll likely be calling from Atlanta. I assume you will fill in Captain Dunn...?" I ask.

"Consider Dunn done", he replies, and there's a small chuckle from the serious Captain Marvel. I think I've made another alliance.

Jacksonville, February 2010

I wake up when I receive a kick to the solar plexus. Presumably I vomited in my sleep, which caused a bit of a stir in the drunk tank at the local jail. My cellmates clearly do not appreciate the mess or the smell. The kick causes me to retch again, but this time it's only dry heaves. I'm fully dehydrated, and haven't eaten in over 48 hours if I'm guessing right. This isn't a first for me. Since my new dedication to getting totally shit-faced each day and all day, I've found myself in the drunk tank on two other occasions. So far, the misdemeanors haven't cost me anything other than twenty-four long hours of *not* being totally drunk and, therefore, causing me to deviate from my goal. That said, I'm pleased with my progress. My skin tone, eye colour, bloated stomach and abdominal pain all point to advancing liver disease. I feel a morbid sense of accomplishment as I silently acknowledge to myself that I am on track. I am drinking myself to death.

The warden of this local jail has heard the commotion and has come to check it out. He finds me sprawled on the floor, and I guess this concerns him. I suppose he doesn't appreciate the potential paperwork associated with violence to inmates. I could use this to my advantage. "Hey buddy... isn't it time I got out of here?"

He ponders this question. Releasing me is an easy way to avoid some paperwork and restore some order to this twelve by fourteen jungle. "You know, you may be right. You were brought in yesterday afternoon on a drunk and disorderly, right?"

"Sounds right," I say unconvincingly. "Name's 'Professor'. Maybe you could check and see when I can get out of here."

"I'll do that. Until then, you just stay away from your friends and keep your nose clean." He turns to my cell mates. "Listen you lowlifes... this man is either going to stay in this cell and make it a smelly hell hole, or you are all going to leave him alone until I get back with release papers. It's up to you." With that he leaves me with a couple of wet naps to wipe my face, then disappears.

My pal reappears about fifteen minutes later, unlocks the cell door and says, "You're free to go, Professor. Pick up your possessions and your court appearance date from the front desk on your way out. And... don't let me see you back here any time soon, you hear?"

"Roger that." I salute, garnering a smirk from my jailer.

I go through the checkout process, noting that it's 1:30, and saunter out into the sunshine. As usual, my first order of business is to return to my stash, get some cash and get drunk. It's a bit of a trek, but I cross the Main Street South bridge and make my way to Treaty Oak Park. I find my stash, get enough cash for a jug and head over to Big Al's.

I'm greeted with the usual disdain from the lard ass. But he accepts my money and I leave with my precious supply of Jack Daniel's. I head back to my spot near the Fuller Warren Bridge, take a quick dip in the St. Johns River then sit back in the sun, tilt my bottle of Jack and let the liquor cascade down my throat.

Other than my few encounters with law enforcement, my days have taken on a familiar pattern. Get cash. Get booze. Get drunk. The occasional swim in the St. Johns is the only form of hygiene I'm practicing now. Food is sporadic and often comes as an after-thought. I'm not above dumpster diving anymore (why waste money on food?). The 'Pink Salt Restaurant and Wine Bar' is conveniently located and, like many upscale eateries, their refuse is often quite good. I've even found half bottles of wine in their dumpsters. Bonus.

I try to piece together the events of yesterday that led to my incarceration. I think I was in the parking lot of the Pink Salt at the time. Some yuppie on lunch saw me stumble out of the dumpster with my fancy 'leftovers', and as he walked by me he decided he should spit on me. Now, normally, if I'm sober, I would just say something smart-assed and proceed on my way. But, being pretty drunk already and in a particularly pissy mood, I decided to spit back. The resulting stain on his designer tie did not sit nicely with him. First he threatened to kill me. Then he said, 'Fuck it. You're not worth the effort'. He climbed into his BMW at that point, gave me the finger, then pulled out his cell phone.

I was consuming my meal by the dumpster, idly

wondering why he'd parked his fancy car in the back laneway of the restaurant, when one of Jacksonville's finest pulled up in his cruiser. He drew himself up to his full six-foot height and came up to me. Without speaking, he threw the remainder of my meal back into the dumpster, then slapped the cuffs on me. The yuppie, who had waited in his car to watch the action, jumped out and started to rant about AIDS, and assault, and pointed to his stained tie. The officer asked me point blank, "Did you do that?"

I responded honestly, pointing to my shirt, "Yeah, but he fired first."

The officer glared at the yuppie, who, on seeing how the conversation was veering from the direction he'd wanted it to go, climbed back into his car, flashed me the finger again, and took off. I saluted similarly at the retreating vehicle. The officer put me in the back of the cruiser saying, "You're going to get a stay in the crow bar motel, where you can sober up. I'll pretend I didn't see or hear about any exchange between you and Mr. Fancy Pants."

That was probably the most interaction with humanity, and the most excitement I'd had (not including with my surly cashier at Big Al's), in over a month. I can't say I miss it. Frankly, people are a distraction from my goal. And incidents like the one that I just encountered only waste my time. Besides, the less interaction I have with humanity, the less likely it is that I'll come upon another child in distress. I've become a vortex, sucking in misery and pain for anyone

I come into contact with. So, best just to not come into contact, and finish what I started over five years ago.

Atlanta, February 2010

I arrive in Atlanta's busy airport after spending time on the plane re-reading the AP wire stories, and studying the map of Atlanta that I'd purchased before leaving Nashville. It looks like the action took place in the southwest part of the city. The only hotel that makes sense for me to stay at is the Fairfield Inn, just off of MLK Boulevard. It takes no time to grab a cab and provide my destination.

The Fairfield Inn isn't posh by any means, but it's tidy and well run. I booked a room on the third floor, which overlooks a nice green space. The king size bed beckons. Air travel always tires me. I stow my carryon in the hall closet atop the luggage rack, slip into a tee shirt and study the Atlanta story again from bed. I decide on my approach for tomorrow morning, then watch a bit of mindless TV before calling it a night.

As I'm channel surfing, I find ESPN is broadcasting a NHL hockey game. Maybe it's the name dropping that the Professor has been doing, but for some reason, I'm looking at the game differently from before. I've always been a fan, but never one to watch it much on TV; the television has never done justice to the pace and intensity of the game. I prefer to go to live games. Anyhow, as I'm watching I start to think of the connections the Professor has created. That's when it hits me. The game on TV is coming from Detroit. The Red Wings versus the Bruins, coming to you from 'Hockey Town USA' as the broadcaster refers to Detroit.

I've already got an inkling that the Professor is from that city, but, maybe there is another line on him... maybe he was involved with organized hockey at some level. It's a line of thought I'll pursue, but, for now, as my eyelids start to droop, I decide to get some shut eye and be prepared to hit the streets of Atlanta tomorrow.

I awaken pretty refreshed around 8.00. After blinking my eyes into focus, I grab the hotel bathrobe and make my way to the bathroom. After a good long shower, I throw on my jeans and a tee shirt. I grab a coffee and danish from the continental breakfast that has been set up in the hotel lobby, then return to my room to make some calls.

My first call is to the Atlanta Fire and Rescue. There is a direct line listed for Medical Services Section.

"Atlanta Fire and Rescue, Emergency Medical Services. How can I direct your call?"

"I'd like to speak with one of your paramedics. His name is Mike Rogers."

"One moment, please."

The line is silent for a minute. Then, I'm greeted with "Fire Station Number 10".
I repeat my request. "Can I speak with Mike Rogers, please?"

"One moment, please." The Atlanta fire department is nothing if not consistent. After a brief moment, I'm finally connected.

"Hello, Mike Rogers here. What can I do for you?"

I'm happy that I caught him on-shift, and after

introducing myself I get right to the point. "I'm wondering if I can have a word with you about an emergency you were first responder to recently. Do you recall tending to a child who'd ingested poison and was carried to your station by a man calling himself 'David Legwand'?"

"Sure, that was just a few weeks ago. Why are you interested?"

"If it's okay with you, I'd like to talk to you about the incident in person. I'd be happy to meet you somewhere convenient. What time does your shift end?"

"Umm, okay. I'm done at noon. How about we meet at Dakota Blue? It's a restaurant just off of Cherokee Avenue."

"Sounds good, see you then. I'll be wearing a black skirt with an off white blouse." Nothing like stoking a man's imagination. I hang up then. I don my hiking boots and head out for a short stroll around the area to stretch my legs and my brain. After Atlanta, where should I go next? And how should I approach the hockey angle?

Returning to my room, I reluctantly change out of my jeans and tee shirt and put on the infamous pencil skirt and my pumps. I style my hair and apply a bit of eye makeup and lipstick. I've never met a male first responder who doesn't respond to this look. I don't have to go over the top, but, I do find if I make an effort it's appreciated, and tends to loosen lips.

I grab a cab and make the 15 minute ride to the

restaurant, arriving a few minutes early. I decide to wait outside the front doors. At twelve fifteen, a blue Chevy Camaro pulls in at the curb and out hops a guy who oozes confidence. This must be my paramedic. He's a looker, no doubt. I catch his eye as he catches mine, and he saunters over, extending his hand.

"Mike Rogers. You must be Joanne."

"I must be," I say with a smile.

He smiles back, making me grin. "How do you like Cuban food?" he asks.

"Well, honestly I'm not that hungry, but I could have a Mojito, and maybe some tortilla chips and salsa."

"Great. I'm starved. Mind if we eat outside? I've been in the station house all shift and could use some fresh air."

"Not at all." We find a table on their patio and place our drink orders. I catch Mike glancing at me several times while he pretends to read the menu. I think my prep time is about to pay dividends.

I launch into my line of questioning. "So... Mike... I read in the newspaper article that you were the first responder at the incident I asked about on the phone. Is that accurate?"

"Well, yes... and no. See, we didn't really respond in the traditional sense. We were not dispatched to the scene. This guy... Mr. Legwand... he actually brought the child to the station."

"Oh... that's interesting. I'll bet that's pretty rare. So, he must've been close to the station then when it happened."

"Yeah. The kid's relative... I think her grandmother... she lives real close to the station. Just over on Park Ave, I forget the house number. Anyway, I told the guy that his effort to carry the little girl over to the station likely saved her life. It would have taken us time to get there, what with the traffic."

"And, how do you know this, I mean the relative's address?" I ask, continuing the informal chat as our food arrives.

"Well, he got a bit jittery at the hospital when I was trying to usher him over to admittance to get the girl's info. That's when he spilled the beans about not being related to her. He told me the grandmother's name ... Annette I think... and her address. Luckily, the grandma, Annette, showed up right around then."

"So, once the girl was admitted... did you find out any specifics about her condition, and what caused it?"

"Well, Mr. Legwand said they thought she'd swallowed something. I told the doctor that, and, apparently when Annette arrived at the hospital, she brought this jar with her that had some of the stuff. The doctor sniffed it and said he believed it was anti-freeze."

"Anti-freeze. Isn't that a bit odd for Atlanta?"

"Well, a bit, I suppose. But, you know, we get the occasional freeze in December and January. And some of these older houses that aren't well insulated, the pipes can freeze and sometimes burst. It isn't too unusual for folks to keep some anti-freeze around, just in case."

"Interesting. So, there was also in the newspaper article a bit about this Mr. Legwand being sought after by the police. What information were you able to share with them?"

"Really not much more than I just shared with you. I talked to a detective Homstead – he asked much the same questions you've just asked. And, like him, I was a bit curious too as to why this guy just sort of vanished. But, that's about all I can tell you."

"And did you talk to the grandmother at all?"

"She was pretty hysterical at first, so no, not right away. But once the doctor told her what he thought had happened, and that the little girl would be okay, she and I talked briefly."

"And, what did she have to say?"

"She asked me where 'the Professor' went. I asked her who she meant... and she explained that was the name that Mr. Legwand went by. Anyhow, she carried on about what a hero he was and how sorry she was that he wasn't around for her to thank him. I kind of felt the same way, but what can you do? I got the impression from her that even though he'd helped her out with odd jobs and so on, that he was a bit of a drinker, so I guess it's not all that unusual for those kind of folks to get the urge to move on."

"That's true I suppose." I finish my Mojito, and even though my new friend Mike hasn't finished his meal I make motions to prepare to leave, thanking him for his information. I can tell he's a bit disappointed that our discussion is ending so quickly, and, bless his heart, he makes a pass at me.

"So, I've told you all I know. What's your story, Joanne? Why are you so interested in this? Maybe we can help each other... Hey, maybe we can make some plans over dinner tonight... what do you say?"

"Well, Mike, I do appreciate the information, and the offer. You're very sweet. But I'm afraid I can't tell you much about my current work, and, also, I really don't like mixing business with pleasure. Sorry, but, maybe when I'm finished with this story I'll look you up again." I hate leaving a man with no hope. His face brightens, he shakes my hand and returns to the Cuban sandwich and Cristal beer he's been working on.

I hail a cab, and as I ride back to the hotel I review what I've learned. First, I now know who I'll contact at the Atlanta Police Department – it's not Detective Murray as the newspaper suggested, it's Detective Homstead. That's not unusual, as the newspaper generally deals with public relations types, while the real detectives working the case stay behind the scenes. Secondly I learned that anti-freeze was the specific toxin that the little girl swallowed. I Google it and learn that anti-freeze becomes dangerous if as little as 100 milligrams is ingested; in a small child a smaller amount could be fatal if not caught quickly. Organ failure starts happening in as little as a few hours. Flora got lucky in many ways: being rushed to the fire station by our Good Samaritan the Professor; then to the hospital thanks to Mystic Mike the paramedic; also grandma having the sense to bring a sample of the suspected toxin to the hospital – identifying what she swallowed would have made it a lot easier for the doctor to treat her. Third, I learned the street and the first name of the little girl's relative, her grandma Annette on Park Avenue. Lastly, not that I needed confirmation, but the alias Mike mentioned confirms we are dealing with the Professor. Three cities... three incidents...one guy. All confirmed.

I arrive back at the hotel and change back into my jeans and tee shirt. I decide to tackle finding the girl's relative first before tracking down Detective Homstead. I think the more I know going into a conversation with the good detective the better.

I don't waste time, and I head out to grab a cab. I ask the cab driver to take me close to Fire Station 10, which was a good call, because Park Avenue is bisected by the freeway. I get out on the corner of Glenwood and Park Avenue and can actually see the back of the fire station from that vantage point. I scan the length of the street and note that it's about three blocks to the end. Without much more to go on, I take a walk, hoping to run into a neighbor who might point me to Annette's house.

Park Avenue is a lovely tree-lined street with neat bungalows and a cobble stone sidewalk. You can tell that the residents all share pride of ownership. About halfway down the street I come to Park Avenue Baptist Church. It's a fairly new building that has a daycare attached to the east end. I'm in luck – I've

167

arrived at a time when parents are starting to pick up their young kids. Lots of car and pedestrian traffic.

I notice a young woman who is holding the hand of a young child, while struggling with a stroller and a crying baby, and simultaneously attempting to heft a bag stuffed with baby accoutrements onto her shoulder with her free hand.

"Here... let me help you," I offer, as I move to take the bag from her.

She looks at me skeptically and begins to protest, but then shrugs in resignation and says, "Okay, thanks."

We start walking north-west and I attempt to break the ice with some small talk. "Must be a handful with these two pre-schoolers."

"You can say that again. Lucky I don't live far. Usually I don't need all this stuff, but I took my baby Caroline for a long walk before I picked up Charlotte from daycare, so I had to be prepared."

"Well, I'm happy to help. My name is Joanne by the way."

"Mallory. Glad to meet you. Thanks for helping me. Did you just move in to the neighborhood? Haven't seen you around."

I've tweaked her suspicion. "No, I'm not from around here. I'm just doing a story for the publication I work for, and I was scoping out the area. I'm actually looking for a lady named 'Annette', who may live around here on Park Avenue. She and her granddaughter were part of a newspaper story recently that caught my eye. Did you hear about that?"

Mallory nods in acknowledgement. "Yeah. Pretty scary that one. After I read it, I did a quick tour of my house and made sure all my cleaning stuff, and anything else this one can get into, was stored away someplace out of reach. You can't turn your back on these scallywags for a minute."

I chuckle at the term. "So true. Anyhow, Mallory, do you know Annette? I'd really like to talk with her."

"Sure I know her. She's babysat my kids on occasion. But after that incident... well... I'm not sure. Maybe if she was looking after them in my house. She really is a sweet lady, but..." Mallory trails off, then returns to the topic. "I guess it can't hurt to tell you where she lives. She's at 78 Park, just a couple of doors down from us."

After a few minutes, we arrive at Mallory's house. I help her as she climbs up the front steps with all her gear, unlocks her door and gathers her things into the foyer of her neat little bungalow, and we say goodbye.

I walk the short distance to number 78 and use the brass knocker on the front door. After a short wait, the door cracks open and a women who appears to be in her early seventies opens the door and eyes me warily.

"Hi", I say. "Are you Annette?"

"That depends. Do you want money, or are you giving away money?"

Her response makes me laugh a little. "Neither. Your neighbor Mallory down the street said I might find you here. I'm following up on the poison incident involving your granddaughter. Do you mind if I come in?"

"Well, what is it you want to know? Are you with the police?" She has a worried look on her face, perhaps nervous that I think she'd been negligent.

"No, I'm not with the police. My name is Joanne Hope and I'm an investigative reporter, looking into the story of the man who helped save your granddaughter." I show her my business card.

"Okay, I guess you can come in then." She opens the door wide enough to let me pass then ushers me into her small, but well-appointed living room. "So, what about the incident are you following up on? And, come to think of it, how did you know that it involved me and my granddaughter? They kept our names out of the paper."

"Finding you is just part of what I do for a living. Should I call you Annette? Or would you prefer Mrs......?"

"I prefer if you call me Mrs. Williams. I know, I'm a little old-fashioned."

I silently congratulate myself as I now have a last name for Annette. "Mrs. Williams, the reason I'm here is I'm working on a follow-up story on the incident. If you don't mind, I'd like to ask you a few questions. I promise, like the newspaper, I can keep your family names out of it."

"I guess it can't hurt. But first can I get you something to drink? Cold tea, lemonade, water, … or something hot?"

"No, thank you. And I'll try not to take much of your time."

"That's okay. Emmaline is still having her nap, so now is as good a time as any to talk."

"Great. So, Mrs. Williams, can you describe what happened that day?"

She sits quietly for a moment while she composes her thoughts. "Well, the Professor was here. He'd helped me with a few handyman jobs, and I was having a problem in the basement. There was some water that kept appearing on the laundry room floor, and a weird noise that I just couldn't figure out. So, he comes up and tells me he found this pump problem and he was going to try to fix it. I really didn't understand much, other than it might cost me some money if he cleaned it up and the pump still didn't work. Anyway, little Emmaline was with us as he explained it all, being quiet… which is pretty unusual for her. I thought maybe she needed a nap, even though it wasn't her regular time. After we chatted, the Professor goes back downstairs to clean out the sump pump.

"I was in the living room reading my book while the Professor did his work in the basement. Emma had wandered down – she was always curious when he was here working on something. I could hear her chattering away, and the Professor was trying not to ignore her saying things like, 'Oh, that's nice…' or 'Oh boy, you

171

must have been excited!'... you know, the type of things you say when you aren't really paying attention to the child, but want to keep her occupied while you go about your business. A little while later, I went into the kitchen to pour myself and the Professor a lemonade, and I see Emmaline lying on the floor! Only, she's not lying still. She's shaking all over, like she's having a fit." Recounting this, Annette's voice is trembling and I see her eyes filling with tears.

She continues, "I try to stop her from shaking... and I'm starting to panic. I don't even know what I said, but suddenly the Professor is there and he's shouting, 'I'm taking her to the fire station!' He picks her up and he's off like Usain Bolt, running out the door and up the street. I'm just in shock, my brain can't comprehend what has happened. I think I stood there frozen for what seems like forever, and then I see that the door under the sink is open and there's a mason jar with a bit of pink fluid in it sitting on the floor. The lid is lying beside the jar. My brain finally activates and I put two and two together. I grab the jar and run out the door with my car keys. I get to the fire station and I can see the paramedic van pulling away with lights flashing. I figure they've got Emmaline, so I follow it to the Grady Medical Center. When I get there I make a beeline for the Emergency admittance desk, and then I see the Professor talking to a paramedic. I hand over the jar of pink stuff to the paramedic and he gets a nurse's attention, who passes it to the doctor who's looking after Emmaline. The Professor was standing back but I went to him and thanked him for what he'd done for Emma. The hospital staff tell me that they believe the liquid is anti-freeze, and they are happy I brought it, because it's going to help them treat her now that they know what she drank. They say she's going to be okay, and you can't believe the relief I feel. Anyhow, by the time I give the front desk the information they need, and the paramedic is speaking with the medical staff, the Professor has vanished. I looked out for him after that, but I never saw him again. That's about all I can tell you."

"That must have been very distressing, Mrs. Williams. Did the police investigate? Were you able to give them any other information?"

"Not that day, no. But they came around the next day and I told them pretty much the same thing as I just told you."

"I'm curious about something. Why was there anti-freeze in your kitchen?"

"Well now, the police asked that very same question. A few years back, we had a nasty cold spell. This is an old house that doesn't do well with real cold temperatures. My toilet got clogged and it turns out it was frozen… I guess where the trap is… at least according to my neighbor. Anyhow, he came over and said he'd pour some anti-freeze down it and see if that might do the trick. I never paid no never mind to exactly what he did, but it worked. I remember him saying afterwards that it looked like the anti-freeze worked, and that he'd leave the rest behind for next time. I guess he just put the remnants under the kitchen sink. I just plumb forgot it was there."

"So, you don't think the Professor brought it with him?"

"No, no, no." Annette paused to think a minute. "He did have a backpack with him, so I guess that's possible. But I really doubt it. He wasn't the sort to cause trouble. He was a drinker, but he really enjoyed talking to Emmaline. No, the anti-freeze was all my fault."

At that, she begins to cry softly, and tears start to flow down her cheeks. I reach for the Kleenex box on the coffee table and she takes one, regaining her composure. "You know, the police asked a lot of the same questions. I got the impression they weren't convinced right off that it was an accident. First they were suspicious of me, if you can believe that, then they seemed to zero in on the Professor. It didn't help that he took off from the hospital and just disappeared."

"Yeah, you know the cops, they're suspicious by nature. It comes with the job I guess. And really, where kids are involved I guess they need to be extra vigilant. Tell me, do you recall the officers' names?"

"Well you're right about being extra vigilant. I can't blame them. Anyhow, it was one detective – his name was Homstead. Big strapping young man. Kind of intimidated me at first, but he was all right. He explained why he was asking all these questions – he said it's routine where a child is involved."

"Well, thank you for sharing this with me, Mrs.

Williams. I know it's not easy to revisit traumatic experiences like that."

She assures me it's no trouble at all. As we are making our way to the door, suddenly a little girl dressed in pink tights and tee shirt comes stumbling out of a door down the hallway, rubbing her eyes. "Nana, who's the lady?"

"Just a friend, dear. You slept well. Do you want to watch some cartoons now?"

"Okay. Bye, nice lady."

She's adorable. Once again, I feel a maternal stirring that surprises me, but at the same time comforts me. I can't believe anyone could ever harm her. But this story has some unsettling aspects. I wave goodbye, and little Emmaline waves back. Annette smiles with pride, then pats my hand and says, "I hope your story teaches people to keep poisons away from kids. I don't want this to happen to anyone else." I assure her I will do my best, thank her for her time, say my goodbye, and take my leave.

My next discussion will be with Detective Homstead. But that can wait until tomorrow. It's been a long day and I need to get back to the hotel and take down some notes on my laptop so I don't forget any details.

Jacksonville, February 2010

I wake up in a cold sweat. After a groggy few minutes, I orientate myself. As I gradually take in my surroundings, I see I'm in a bed... clean sheets, an intravenous drip. As I slowly make my way to a sitting position, the unmistakable feel of the open back of a hospital gown sends a shiver down my spine. So, I know I'm in a hospital, but I have no clue how I got here... or even where here is. As I pause my hazy scrutiny of the room, I close my eyes and start to think back. What do I remember? I remember spending the night (or at least part of it) at a shelter – a rarity since my arrival in Jacksonville. I just wanted a mattress and some warmth. After downing most of my jug from Big Al's, I'd stumbled over the bridge to the shelter on the other side of the river. I remember raising a stink because they confiscated the remnants of my bottle. Then I recall getting tossed out a few hours later, after going on a rant and demanding my bottle back.

Then it comes to me. I recall something had snapped in me. It was as if I had been looking over an abyss, not unlike that day from years ago. Only this time, it wasn't grief I was feeling. It was red hot anger. Angry with myself, at my failures, at my cowardly self-preservation. I'm here because, for the first time in my life on the streets, I decided alcohol and the occasional reefer wasn't enough. I needed to expand my destructive ways. I had stumbled back across the bridge, retrieved my stash and headed for the San

Marco subway station, where I knew I could find some something more potent (lethal?).

      The meth, the meth heads... it's all coming back. I don't recall the guy's name. Just another mangy homeless meth user. I asked him where to score, and he looked at me skeptically. Then, I remember him saying, "I might have some. You got cash?" Still very drunk, I showed him a wad of cash. He pulled out a pipe and I had my first experience. After another hit, I remember hearing a cruel laugh. I'm incapacitated. I'm so high, I can't move. I'm laughing too... but not like he is. I'm laughing because for the first time in years, I'm certain I can do it. I can kill myself. It would be easy. Hell, maybe this guy with the cruel laugh can help me. He is helping me!

      "No, I'm not going to kill you. I'm just going to help myself to that fat wad of cash you're flashing around. Really man, bad move on your part. How about another hit? You seem to be enjoying yourself." Another hit off the pipe, and that's the last I remember.

      And now here I am. I'm weak, but not so weak that I don't know I have to get out of here. I try to climb off the bed, and fail miserably. I find the call button and press it. Maybe I can get some help. A few minutes later a nurse and a doctor appear. The doctor (I assume she's a doctor, given the stethoscope hanging around her neck) apprises me over a clip board. "Well, you made it. We weren't sure you would. I guess you don't read the newspaper, huh?"

      "Sometimes I read it, but usually I just sleep on

it."

"Well, sir, you are lucky. We've had a rash of nasty overdoses lately. Turns out there is a bad batch of meth circulating. You caught some and would likely have died had it not been for an early morning commuter finding you near the station in a pool of your own urine and vomit. He thought you were dead. Phoned it in anonymously, then likely hopped the subway to work. Police showed up, found a pulse and called an ambulance for assistance. You are now at Baptist Medical Center."

She's filled in quite a few blanks for me. Ironic that a Good Samaritan found me, saved my life, then vanished. I wish he hadn't bothered. But it seems I may have found a shortcut to my end goal. Now I just need to get out of here. As if reading my mind the doctor says, "You're staying put for forty-eight hours. State mandate. Don't even think about trying to leave before then." To punctuate the finality of this statement, the doctor and nurse both pivot and leave my bedside as abruptly as they'd arrived.

I sink back into the bed, resigned to my current situation. I'm not sure I can handle forty-eight hours sober, but given I don't feel too bad at that point, I'm pretty sure that the intravenous drip isn't just saline solution. Maybe they figured out I'm a drunk as well as an aspiring meth user and they're trying to bring me down gently. Either way, as I drift in and out of consciousness, it's obvious I'm not going anywhere. I'm physically not capable. It is also crystal clear to me that

maybe I need to consider meth as part of my plan.
After all, that lethal dose is still out there. Maybe it's a
bit like Russian roulette. A grim, mirthless smile creases
my face. Either way, it increases my odds.

Atlanta, February 2010

I'm awake early. Too early. But my mind is racing and I can't help it. I now have three confirmed cases where our mysterious man arrives on the scene just in time to save a child in a life threatening situation. In each case, the man disappears, using the name of a hockey player as his alias. In the first two cases, we have the aura of drugs in the picture. In St. Louis he frequented a park known as a drug dealer haven. In Nashville, he's Johnny-on-the-spot while a young mother is overdosing – from bad heroin that was also found in St. Louis. I wonder if this latest episode in Atlanta has a drug angle? My mind spins. I keep returning to the Big Question.

Is the Professor a hero or a villain? Everyone I've spoken with who's had any direct interaction with him seems to believe without a doubt that he's a hero. But it's hard to ignore the fact that these don't seem to be isolated incidents. Could the guy be on some weird alcohol and drug-fuelled killing spree, with these three failing at the last moment? Of course the scenarios all end with the same ultimate question: why? I doubt if the Atlanta City PD can answer that question, but it's time to connect with Detective Homstead to find out what questions he can answer.

I check the clock sitting on the bedside table and I'm relieved to see it's now a little after 8.00. After a quick shower, a room service breakfast, and a review of the stories on my laptop, I start my search for Detective Homstead. Based on the map that the city has conveniently placed online, the action all took place in police 'Zone-5'. The directory has a main number for Zone-5, which I call.

"You have reached Atlanta Police Service, Zone 5 Precinct. If this is an emergency, please hang-up and call 911, otherwise stay on the line and an officer will be with you as soon as possible." Musak fills my ears. Gentle wind instruments doing a soothing rendition of a tune made famous by Willy Nelson, 'Always on My Mind.' How appropriate. I'm finding this investigation is always on my mind. Finally after a few repeats and several lost hair follicles, the line comes alive.

"Sergeant Debrusk. How can I direct your call?"

"Hello. I'd like to speak with Detective Homstead please."

"Regarding what?"

"It's personal." Sometimes I find this answer gets a quicker response than introducing myself as a journalist. This is one of those times. Without hesitation, I'm patched through to Detective Homstead.

"Homstead" is his clipped one word greeting.

"Good morning, Detective Homstead. My name is Joanne Hope. I'm an investigative journalist working on a story that concerns a case your name has been attached to. I believe you are looking for a man in connection with a little girl named Emmaline, who ingested a toxic substance and required medical treatment. The man goes by the name David Legwand."

There is a pause as he considers his response. I'm sure he is thinking that the media didn't have the little girl's name, nor did it release his name as the detective working the case. So how did I find out? I'm hoping that tweaking his curiosity will garner me an audience with him. Finally, he responds, "Well, you seem to be well informed, Ms. Hope. Maybe you have some information that could help the investigation. A tit for tat, so to speak." Bingo. Got him.

"That sounds good to me. How about I come down to the precinct? I can be there in less than an hour."

More hesitation. I think he realizes I've manipulated him a bit, but he's not about to walk away from what is likely the only call about the disappearance of David Legwand that he's had. "Okay. Let's say eleven a.m. this morning ... and here at the precinct is good." He abruptly hangs up.

I arrive at the station just before eleven. The sergeant working the front desk is Debrusk, the same one who patched me through to Detective Homstead. He eyes me with undisguised hostility as I introduce myself as the detective's eleven o'clock meeting. I'm guessing the detective gave him a small dressing down for patching through a journalist directly to him instead of sending me to media relations. Oh well. Too bad. I'm not here to make pals.

After a brief delay, a short, slightly overweight and balding man appears from behind the smoked glass partition that separates the 'greeting' area of the precinct from the detectives' work space. He takes me in head to toe and I can tell he likes what he sees. He extends his hand in greeting. "Joanne Hope? I'm Detective Homstead. Nice to meet you. I did some checking… nice work on that prostitution ring in Fargo." His hand is beefy. Thankfully it's dry.

"Thank you, Detective." I have to admit it pleases me when my reputation precedes me, and I can parlay a positive reception into information.

Pleasantries dispensed with, he leads me to an interrogation room. I pull out my phone. "I assume you will be recording our conversation. I'll do the same, unless you have objections."

"By all means, be my guest." He starts his recording, and begins, "So, first question for you. How did you find out the girl's name and my name? That wasn't in the papers."

"Really, Detective, does that matter? And besides, I'm not about to divulge sources, even in something as trivial as this. Now, my first question. Given you've likely followed up with all the relevant players by now, do you still view any of what happened as suspicious? Or was our Mr. Legwand just in the right place at the right time?"

"Truth is, I was about to close the case. Some drunks will lace their booze with anti-freeze to stretch their supply. It's cheap and readily available. But, that's a pretty thin connection. So, unless you have more information about Mr. Legwand or this case, I have no reason at this point to believe there was any foul play involved."

I can see that Detective Homstead is not as pliable as I had first believed. I will have to *give* in order to *get*. "No, I don't know Mr. Legwand, or where to find him. I was hoping you'd have information in that regard. But, let's not tap dance anymore."

"Agreed, let's not. Tell me, why is a Pulitzer nominated journalist looking for a homeless guy? I mean, I guess it's a feel good story. He saved a kid, right? But you could find that kind of story just about anywhere. Why here, why this guy?"

"All right, Detective. I'll come clean. Mr. Legwand has gone by other aliases and currently has open missing person cases in two other jurisdictions: Nashville and St. Louis. In both of those cities, he's been involved in incidents where a child has been rescued from a dangerous situation, but then he vanishes." That gets his attention. Big time.

"So, what you're telling me is that Mr. Legwand, or whatever his real name is, has a history of heroics followed by disappearance. Okay. I guess I won't be closing this case. I don't know if I should be happy about this or not, but one thing for sure... you've got my ear. What else can you tell me about these other two cases?"

"Look, let's both save ourselves some time. Why don't we set up a conference call with the detectives working the missing person files in Nashville and St. Louis? We can all compare notes. But, before we do that, can you fill me in on what you've done in

184

trying to locate Mr. Legwand?"

Homstead seems to be satisfied with the idea of speaking with fellow detectives. He's candid, finally. "Well, we spoke with the grandmother... Annette Williams. She put us onto another lady, goes by the name of Doris, who was kind of the neighborhood maintenance organizer. She'd line up work for the Professor, which was the name Annette and Doris used for Mr. Legwand."

"Do you know where the Professor and Doris met?"

"She would catch up with him on a park bench near Kelly Street most mornings. That's where he'd sleep it off, if he didn't go to the Central Night Shelter."

"Oh. So, you connected him to a shelter as well... and let me guess – they have no idea where he's gone."

"You guess correct. "

"It seems we may be at a dead end, location wise. Anything else you can tell me about the man?"

"Really not much. He was a heavy drinker. Occasional marijuana smoker. Basically kept his nose clean, made some pocket money and supported his addiction to alcohol. One of the drug dealers that hangs around the shelter knew him, called him 'Professor Do-Gooder' when we talked to him."

"So Legwand wasn't using drugs, but he was known to this drug dealer. You got a name for the dealer?"

"Yeah, Rudy. He's got a long sheet, but has

never been caught with any large quantity of product. A bit player and a douche bag, but I don't think he's lying. He says he has no idea where our man is."

"Hmm. Okay. Well, that name... 'the Professor'... in case there was any doubt, we are talking about the same guy in St. Louis and Nashville. Same description, same nickname. We have two of your colleagues to bring in to a conference call – that would be Captain Dunn with the St. Louis force and Captain Marvel with the Nashville PD. Both have open missing person cases for the guy. They both know I'm in Atlanta following his trail, and they'll be expecting a call."

"Whoa. That's some heavy shit. Two captains both running shotgun on this? Seems like overkill, to this lowly detective."

"Yeah, well... we have three suspicious cases involving children, across multiple states, so barring involvement by the FBI we need some heavy hitters. You won't be intimidated, will you, Detective?" As expected, the mention of potential FBI involvement got his attention. Appealing to his sense of machismo with the 'intimidation' innuendo certainly didn't hurt either.

"Don't insult me. No, I will not be intimidated. In fact, I'm going to talk to my captain right now. He might want to play poker too. Let me get Sergeant Debrusk to set up a conference call. You have any time that doesn't work for you?"

"I'm available twenty-four, seven," I respond, hoping this call will happen sooner rather than later, but not during the wee hours of the morning when I need my beauty sleep.

"Okay. I'll be in touch."

I head out and grab a quick bite to eat, perusing my emails and the news while scarfing back a chicken salad sandwich on rye, hold the onions. As I finish up, my phone rings and Sergeant Debrusk informs me the conference meeting is set up for this afternoon at two o'clock. I'm happy with the speed this is moving.

I return to the precinct just before two and am greeted this time by Detective Homstead and his superior, Captain Freeman. The captain is almost a carbon copy of his detective. Stalky, with a slight paunch and a receding hair line. He also gives me the same look that the detective gave me early in the day. A combination of curious assessment and just a little bit of lecherous male hormone. Nothing I'm not used to.

I'm ushered into a conference room where the grim Sergeant Debrusk has set up a speaker phone and is busily dialling the conference call number. After a few minutes of technical chicanery, the other participants, Captains Dunn and Marvel, join the call. Greetings made, we get right down to business.

Freeman starts the conversation, "Captains, thank you both for joining us. And, also thank you for sending the case briefs to Detective Homstead. I'd like to start, if you don't mind, by listing the common factors in all three cases. Homstead, can you summarize for us?"

Homstead is flustered, not thinking this would be his show, given that he's the junior officer. So much for not being intimidated. But he regains his composure and starts to list case particulars that fit into the pattern.

"All three cases involve a child between the ages of one and three years. Our missing guy, nicknamed 'the Professor', seems to be Johnny-on-the-spot, and rescues these children from life threatening situations while the parent or guardian is distracted, or in the case of Nashville, dead. Shortly after saving the child, the Professor skips town, after giving a new alias to bystanders. The alias used is always a former NHL hockey player. That's about it. Did I miss anything?"

Dunn and Marvel both seem satisfied with the synopsis. I clear my throat, and Homstead and Freeman both look at me with a degree of suspicion and veiled hostility. I guess they aren't used to civilian participation, and they certainly aren't used to that civilian being a member of the fifth estate and a woman. Nevertheless, I push on.

"Some minor details. First, the Professor doesn't use just any NHL player name. In the St. Louis case, he identified himself as Gordon Howe from Detroit. When I interviewed one of his drinking pals, Joey, he said that he believed the Professor had come to St. Louis via Detroit. The same pattern applies to Nashville, where he used the alias Brett Hull from St. Louis. Then onto Atlanta where he identified himself as David Legwand from Nashville. So, he's leaving breadcrumbs, pointing back to his previous city. I don't know what that means, if it's intentional or not, but it's a pattern, and also lends some credence to Joey's hypothesis that he might have started his journey in Detroit. Second, we know our man is a drinker. But there also seems to be a tinge of drug involvement. Given the overdose of Jane Doe in Nashville, that's a no brainer. But in St. Louis and Atlanta there also is the indication of drug use and/or contact with drug dealers. And, lastly, in each case the witnesses describe him the same way: smart, resourceful, kind, and humble. Not a trouble-maker. He's not your typical homeless alcoholic. I don't know if this paints him in a positive light, or if this means he's a master manipulator, but anyone who has come into contact with him seems to think he's incapable of harming a soul."

There is a pause as the various law enforcement officers digest this additional information. Captain Freeman, seated beside me, is the first to speak. "Okay. Thanks for that, Ms. Hope. But now that it appears we all agree on the salient facts of our related cases, let's also agree on what we don't know. Three things come to mind. Most importantly, we don't know the Professor's current location. Is he still somewhere in Atlanta or has he moved on? Next, we have the possibility that he's from Detroit... but we don't know that for a fact. Last, if we think that there is the possibility of foul play with these children, we've established means and we've established opportunity in all cases, but we have zero ideas around motive." The disembodied voices on the conference call chime in their agreement.

Again, I have to be the one to point out another mystery. "One more thing we don't know. Why use NHL players as aliases? Is there some connection to hockey that might help us figure out who this guy really is?"

There is a grudging acknowledgement that, although this may be a seemingly insignificant detail, it is also one of the few details we do know about the Professor. He has a connection to hockey. But what is that connection?

Captain Dunn speaks next. "All right. We know what we know and we also know what we don't know. The question is, what next? I, for one, am still not convinced we need FBI involvement at this point even though the incidents occurred in different states. But, having said that, their resources could help expedite our search." There is a bit of back and forth on this topic, but I know before they are done chatting exactly where this conversation will land. Nobody wants to have the FBI involved. It would be a disaster for all of their careers if it turned out the Professor was some kind of nasty child abuser and they had let him walk away from their various jurisdictions. It would make much more sense to keep this under wraps until the Professor is found and they have a chance to interrogate him.

I listen quietly, then make my point. "Given that I'm the one who connected the dots here, it's only fair that I get full access to all information. Captains Dunn and Marvel... you guys already agreed we had a deal. Captain Freeman, are you onside?" The unstated threat of me calling the FBI does not need to be articulated. Freeman agrees and we move onto the next topic.

"All right, we agree on holding off on FBI involvement," Marvel says to nobody in particular. "What are the loose threads we want to grab onto to try to unravel this?"

Detective Homstead, who has mostly been quiet since his case synopsis, speaks up. "To me, I think we need to widen the search. I've pretty much exhausted all leads in Atlanta, so given his history of travel I'm pretty sure he's flown the coop."

I speak up, and add some parameters. "I agree with Detective Homstead. And, I think based on his history, we should consider bringing Florida authorities into the loop. He's been migrating south, which shouldn't surprise us. If you're going to be homeless, you might as well be somewhere warm."

Freeman agrees to take on that task and get the ball rolling. "I have contacts in some of the bigger metro PDs in Florida and Louisiana. It won't be a problem to get them to play ball and put out a missing persons alert."

That leaves a thread that has been on my personal to-do list for weeks. "I'm going to do some digging to see if we can confirm the Professor was in Detroit at some time."

Dunn speaks up, "You seem to have a talent for following bread crumbs, so I have no doubt if there is a connection, you will find it. But, I think I speak for all of us when I insist that you share whatever you find. I can help you with Detroit PD if you require their assistance."

Dunn and the others remain a blend of suspicion and cooperation. They are not anxious to expand the official search unless absolutely necessary, for fear of drawing attention from the FBI and/or their superiors. I don't think they have done shoddy police work, but I have no idea what the internal politics of their offices look like. I surmise that each of the captains are trying to manage the situation so that should there be conclusive evidence of wrong doing, they can each claim a role in helping to uncover the larger picture and, hopefully, be part of the apprehension of the perpetrator. I agree to their request. I need them to cooperate as much as they need me.

The call breaks up with a general agreement to have a follow-up call in seventy-two hours, regardless of progress. I'm pleased about this because, as I'm all too aware, the clock is ticking. While I never committed to meeting any deadline, I have the feeling that Jerome is starting to get anxious. And, I do feel I owe him – he's given me a very long leash and it's time to reward his trust. Tony's always anxious, and would have pulled me in long ago if not for Jerome.

Part Three

"To err is human; to forgive, divine." – Alexander Pope

Jacksonville, February 2010

I'm released from hospital, and not a moment too soon. This is the first time in many years that I've been unable to drink myself into a coma every day. The visions that haunted me during semi-lucid, hungover times are increased ten-fold as I find myself in the unfamiliar situation of sobriety. All the feelings of guilt, self-loathing and anxiousness roll over me like a recurring tsunami. A pounding behind my temples conspires with the bright light streaming in from the window to complete the torture started in earnest by my own psyche.

After being lectured to about the dangers of alcohol and drug abuse and the unfortunate state of my liver, I'm handed information about substance abuse programs in the area and sent merrily on my way out the front door. Presumably, my tab paid by the state, I'm free to go. Which means I'm free to get back on track in my quest to end this miserable life. Silently thanking whoever it was who inspired me to split my savings into multiple stashes, I make a beeline to the stash that is only a few blocks away from the hospital, and then to Big Al's. I arrive just as the Elephant Man is flipping the sign on the door from 'Closed' to 'Open'. He greets me with his usual surly expression, mixed with some surprise. I'm guessing that he had assumed he'd seen the last of me given my last couple days of no-show. I make my way quickly to the spirits section of his establishment and select a jug of Jim Beam. It's all I can do not to guzzle from the bottle as I make my way to the cash register and extract cash from the roll I've produced from my backpack. My hand trembles and my fingers fumble as I throw some bills on the counter and take my bottle from Godzilla. After muttering, 'keep the change', I bolt from the store.

On my way to the shores of the St. John River, I fold back the paper sack that 'hides' the golden liquid from prying eyes, remove the cap from the bottle and chug back three large gulps. The burn down my throat is glorious; the warmth in my belly luxurious. The tremors in my hands start to slow within seconds. The taste lingers in my mouth and I can barely contain my pleasure as I walk the remaining few blocks and assume my old position in the undergrowth by the riverside. My 'home' so to speak. As I recline on the shipping pallets and blanket that serve as my bed, I take the bottle from the paper bag and tip it back again, now experiencing the euphoria that a short time ago seemed unattainable. As my mind settles into the numbness I'd grown accustomed to, but was forced to forego for forty-eight unbearable hours, I start to mentally retrace the events that put me in the hospital bed.

Meth. Meth put me in the hospital. And, I know sometime during that trip I'd considered trying to hunt down more of it, as a means to an end. But now that I'm cradling my magnificent bottle of Jim Beam, that idea has lost its luster. Nodding to myself, I decide I'm going back to my original plan. The hours spent in the hospital are a minor setback. While it's true that the liver has a regenerative ability that is often described as miraculous, I'm sure my liver will not be able to withstand the onslaught I have planned for it, despite the brief reprieve.

Next, I think about who I talked to in the hospital. My anonymity might have been compromised; however, I know that whomever I identified myself as (hopefully the Professor?) there is no corroborating evidence to be found anywhere. If I had died, I would have died John Doe.

My mind at ease, and the visions of the past erased (or at least temporarily beaten down), I settle back with another pull from the bottle. All is right in my world. I need only continue on this course for several more months before sliding peacefully into oblivion.

Atlanta and Detroit, February 2010

After a testy conversation with Tony where he reminded me I only had one more week to make our publishing deadline, I decide that I should spend some time searching the AP wire again to see if the good Professor had left any semblance of a trail in the fine city of Detroit. I zero in on the timeframe mid-2004 to mid-2006, recalling that the Professor's drinking pal Joey mentioned he'd known the Professor for a couple of years prior to the 2007 incident in St. Louis. Using the AP Search function, I enter Detroit as the location, and initially try key phrases 'child rescue' and 'toddler rescue', both coming up with no useful matches. I then change tack and focus on the Professor himself. What did I know about him that might harvest results? Judging by the photos and descriptions of him, I guessed his approximate age as mid-thirty to forty. Allowing for elapsed time, I search for variations of 'missing man' and 'missing male', with approximate age ranges, race. Again, I'm not getting the results I hope for. Then it dawns on me. I'd read somewhere that there is a national registry of missing persons. Perhaps that registry has entered the digital world.

I abandon my AP wire search and use Google search to see if I can find a link to the registry database. "Eureka!" I exclaim to myself. Google provides a link to the 'NamUs' National Missing and Unidentified Persons System. I click on the 'About' reference which appears on the site's main page to get an idea as to the validity of the database. It's impressive. In collaboration with the National Institute for Justice, the National Forensic Science Technology Center and the Occupational Research and Assessment center developed and launched the NamUs Unidentified Persons database in 2007. The following year, the NamUs Missing Persons database was launched, and in 2009, the two databases were connected for automatic case comparisons, expanding the power of NamUs to make associations between missing and unidentified persons. I had hit the motherlode of missing persons doing one Google search. I pause to consider my newfound feeling of humility. How could I, as an investigative journalist, be so myopic in the way I've been looking at this story and the resources I've been using? No wonder Tony is not enthralled with me these days. Instead of spending thousands of dollars hopscotching across the country, perhaps I would have been more efficient, and effective, had I started with my new best friend (or worst enemy?), the Google search engine.

I shake off this strange feeling of ineptitude and take a closer look at NamUs's capabilities. There is a basic search feature that allows entry of just the state and county where your person might have gone missing. I try this and get a list of over 600 names; but it also includes columns listing personal information such as the person's name, sex, age, race, last date of contact, and physical characteristics. I notice that there is an 'advance search' button. I click on this and am happy to see a very detailed search screen that allows you to zero in on your target.

Refining my search, I specify my missing person as a 'Caucasian' 'Male' with a last date of contact between July 1, 2004 and July 1, 2006. Unfortunately I'd only be guessing on things like hair colour, eye colour, weight and height, but I mentally file this as a possible future refinement should I need it. I need not worry, however, because as the search results come up I see that I am only looking at six potential matches for the elusive man we know as the Professor. And, of those six, one is most promising. Aged early thirties at his time of disappearance from Flint, Michigan. His name is Geoffrey Talbot.

I click on the name and I'm redirected to details about Geoffrey Talbot, including a photo of him taken around the time he went missing. It is indisputable. I'm sure it's him.

My heart is pounding. The abstraction known as the Professor is now the reality known as Geoff Talbot. Or, rather the potential reality. I still don't know much more about our mystery man. For that, I consider a return to the AP Wire database. But, then I check myself. Google is very powerful; perhaps it will provide answers. I return to the Google search bar and type 'Geoffrey' and 'Talbot'. I'm overwhelmed with a return of over three million matches. Clearly, I need to narrow my search parameters. I refresh the search and type 'Geoffrey', 'Talbot' and 'Michigan'. This time, I'm still confronted with over eight hundred thousand results. Clearly, there is something about this search engine I don't understand. I scan the first several entries and realize that the search engine returns many partial results. For example, I see entries for Geoffrey Talbot who owns a cheese factory near Lake Michigan. Geoff Talbot who was born in Michigan but who died in 1846 in Yorkshire England. Frustrated, I decide it's likely my unfamiliarity with the tool that is causing the problem, so I return to my tried and true AP Wire database.

I log into the database and type "Geoffrey Talbot". The search engine allows you to enter separate parameters to include in your search by using a plus sign, then the additional criteria in parentheses, so I include "+ Michigan". The default setting is to sort the resulting hits starting with the most recent news item and moving backwards in time.

This time, I'm successful. The first story I find is from the Flint Journal, dated September 6, 2005. As I read it, I can barely contain my excitement.

> *'Police are concerned by the disappearance of a thirty-four year old man, Geoffrey Talbot. Talbot, a respected teacher at Powers Catholic High School and coach of the Flint Flyers senior high school hockey club, was last seen in the school parking lot one day prior to the start of the school year.*
>
> *"I spotted Geoff and asked him if he was ready for the upcoming year," his colleague and fellow*

teacher at the school, Derek Ross, noted. "He looked at me, or more like he looked through me, and it was as if he didn't understand, so I repeated my question. Then he just got in his car and took off without saying a word. It seemed very strange behaviour for Geoff."

His car was later found in a Walmart parking lot on Corunna Rd.

Sources confirm that Talbot had recently been released from Genesee County Mental Health facility where he had been receiving treatment following the death of his wife, Martha Talbot, and their two year daughter, Jennifer, in May of this year.

Police do not suspect foul play, but are concerned that Talbot may be in distress. Anyone with information concerning his whereabouts is asked to contact the Genesee County Sheriff's Office at 585-345-3000.'

A picture of Geoffrey Talbot is included with the article, and it is the same picture used in the posting to the NamUs Missing Persons database. A chill runs down my spine. I can feel myself getting tantalizingly close to Geoff Talbot, alias the Professor, without leaving my hotel room in Atlanta.

Scrolling back in time, I find another article dated June 1, 2005. However, this wasn't a newspaper article per se; it is an obituary.

> *'Condolences are extended to Geoffrey Talbot,
> following the death of his beloved wife Martha
> (nee Burke), born February 7, 1971, and their
> daughter Jennifer, born May 8, 2003. A funeral
> service will not be held for Martha and Jennifer,
> at the request of Mr. Talbot. Instead, friends
> who wish to do so are asked to donate to the
> World Wildlife Fund in their names. Martha and
> Jennifer will be laid to rest June 5 in Martha's
> home town of Newberry, Michigan.'*

Other than some random blurbs in the sports
pages of the Flint Journal following a win or loss by the
Flint Flyers, this is the last of the articles of any interest
about Geoffrey. I have more questions now than
answers. First amongst the questions is: why is this
obituary so sparse, so bleak and so unemotional? It
appears as though Martha and Jennifer did not really
have a life other than their connection to Geoffrey
Talbot. It looks as though a funeral home had written
the obituary. Certainly nobody close to the deceased
ones had written it. Why is the obit so impersonal?

Of course, the lack of any details as to the
causes of death also creates a tsunami of questions,
some disturbing. Was Geoff involved in their deaths in
some way? If so, how? Given that the first article I read
mentioned a stay in a mental health facility after the
deaths of his wife and daughter, the question is, were

there mental health issues before the deaths? Despite my deepest desire to *not* visit Michigan in the middle of February, I can't see a way around it. Time to pack.

There is an airport in Flint, Michigan, but no direct flights from Atlanta. I opt for an American Airlines direct flight to the airport most convenient to Flint, the Detroit Metro Airport, which leaves in two hours. I arrive early at the airport, so that I can take some time to make a few calls from the comfort of the first class lounge before boarding the plane. Yes, I'm going first class. I'm sure Tony will have kittens when he reviews my travel expenses, but when you've been on the road for six plus weeks, the occasional perk keeps you going. I settle back with a martini and place a call to Captain Freeman of the Atlanta PD.

"Freeman," is his single word phone greeting.

"Captain Freeman, it's Joanne Hope. I've got some information for you. Our boy was definitely in the Detroit area – Flint to be precise. Turns out there is a 2005 missing person case, attached to a high school teacher slash hockey coach named Geoffrey Talbot."

Freeman replies quickly, "Well. So do you think that's his real name? Or another alias?"

I'm momentarily thrown by the question. It seems obvious to me that it's as real a name as we're going to find. Trying to hide the sarcasm from my voice I then respond, "Well, he was employed under that name, which would suggest a paycheck, taxes, and all the other accoutrements of being a real person."

Freeman, doubling down on dumb questions

203

asks, "Are you in Michigan now? How did you find this information?"

"Funny you should ask. It seems I've been running around the country trying to get a handle on this guy, when all I really needed to do was a couple of online searches. Have you ever heard of 'NamUs'?"

Another awkward pause, then finally, "The name sounds familiar."

"The National Institute for Justice, along with forensics and some other organization created this database over a year ago, which allows you to enter and search profiles of missing people. I'm sure someone in your department must be familiar with it."

"Hmm... yeah, that's probably why it sounds familiar. I think our forensics team has checked it out, maybe even had a tutorial or something."

"Okay, well I suggest you go talk to them. And do you think you could also fill in Captain Dunn and Captain Marvel?"

A slightly sheepish response, "Sure, I can do that."

I continue, "One more thing. Are you sitting down? It turns out that Geoffrey Talbot spent time in a mental health facility in Michigan after the deaths of his wife and two year old daughter in 2005."

I can hear, and almost visualize, the sigh. I surmise the good captain has visions of FBI agents invading his precinct. Then, unexpectedly, he changes subjects back to my online sleuthing. "You mentioned that this database NamUs was initiated by the National

Institute for Justice. So, not the FBI. Interesting."

These guys never cease to amaze me. Their jurisdictional pissing contests seem to know no bounds. I'm now starting to think maybe I should call the FBI. But, I will hear him out.

"Sure... I guess that's interesting, if you are in law enforcement... which I'm not. Can you give me a reason why we shouldn't be calling the FBI at this point?"

"Truth is, off the record, we probably should. But, as you recall, we widened the search for our guy. I contacted departments in Mississippi and Florida, and I promised my interstate colleagues in those states that if they started to look for the Professor we'd keep the FBI out of it. Let's give them at least the courtesy of seventy-two hours from now, and if nothing turns up, we all present the facts to our friends in the agency. Agreed?"

I'm torn, but in the end I agree. Just before hanging up I remind him to fill in Dunn and Marvel. We end the call just as my boarding call is announced.

The plane ride is uneventful, but I have to admit I enjoy being spoiled in first class, even if it's only for a few hours. As I'm exiting the plane it dawns on me that my attire of suit jacket, fleece, and windbreaker are simply not going to be suitable for the nasty cold of a Michigan winter. Luckily, the airport has a splendid shopping concourse, where I'm able to purchase some stylish winter boots and a knee length down-filled jacket. I should be warm enough, and I'll look good too.

Who said winter has to be all bad?

I make my way to the Avis counter and rent a Chevy Equinox. I have no idea what the weather for the next few days will be, but I think a little four wheel drive SUV should handle it. I also purchase a map of Detroit and surrounding environs that includes a map of Flint. Since the only lead I have is the school that the teacher Derek Ross mentioned, Powers Catholic High School, home of the Flint Flyers, I decide that will be my first stop. I call ahead and after a brief wait, I speak with Samantha Ing, the principal, who agrees to meet with me over the lunch hour. I didn't tell her much, just that I was doing a story about missing persons and wanted to include a bit about Geoff and the impact on the school. Somewhat of a white lie, but who's to say I won't include Mr. Talbot's teaching background as part of my story?

As I leave the comfy confines of Detroit Metro Airport, I'm greeted with a gust of cold air that leaves me gasping. I pull the zipper up the collar of my new jacket to cover my neck and mouth, raise my furry hood, and make my way through the car rental parking lot to my Avis Equinox. Not exactly a Range Rover, but it looks serviceable. Most importantly, I turn the key and it starts. I wonder how often the cars left out here in this bitter cold to just die a slow and painful death?

I pull away and enter the Detroit highway system, destined for Flint. The drive takes a little over an hour and I arrive just in time for the school's lunch break, finding a spot marked 'visitor', close to the entrance.

After going through a metal detector, I see a sign for the principal's office. Samantha's door, however, is guarded by a severe woman who has her name prominently displayed on her desk as Ms. Frownton. If ever there was a name that fit a person's 'at rest face', this would be the one. 'Ms. Frownie Face' speaks on the telephone announcing my arrival and out from a frosted glass door pops a smiling, petite woman in her mid- to -late thirties. Her facial features are an exotic mix, giving her an Asian/African look. A slim build is shown to her advantage in a well-fitted black pantsuit with a gold coloured blouse and black low-heeled shoes. I assume this is Samantha Ing. Ms. Frownie Face throws a disapproving look towards her, which makes me instantly like her. We shake hands.

"Hello, Ms. Hope. What a pleasure to meet you. I'm a fan of your writing."

"That's so nice to hear, especially from an educator." I'm liking her more all the time. "Please, call me Joanne."

"And I'm Samantha. Let's head over to the staff lounge. You can meet some of Geoff's colleagues."

"That would be great. But before we get too much further, could we chat in your office? I'm not sure how much of this should remain private." I really don't want to discuss Geoff's case in front of Ms. Frownie Face.

"Of course," she responds, closing her office door behind us.

"I need to tell you a bit more about my story. It's not really about missing persons, in general. It's about Geoff in particular. You see, over the course of the last several years, he's been the central figure in some interesting events."

I have her attention. "When you say 'interesting' I hope you mean that in a positive sense."

"I hope so too. That is part of the reason I'm here. I need to understand more about Geoff. What kind of man he is. And, I need to know about his wife and child, and their deaths."

Just by uttering these words, I can see a change come over Samantha. I read the emotions of pain and sadness as they transform her face from vibrant and exuberant to reflective and downcast in seconds. She shakes her head, her voice lowers. "That was almost seven years ago. But it still feels like it happened yesterday. I can't tell you how painful it was to watch Geoff suffer through that. Martha and Jenny were his world. When he lost them, he just couldn't function anymore. It's still painful for us here."

"So... do you still want to do this? I'm really sorry. I can see I've brought back some bad memories."

"No. Really, that's okay. If I can help Geoff in any way, by telling you his story from my perspective, I will be happy to do so. But I'd really prefer to do this off of school grounds."

"Sure. That would be fine. Let me buy you lunch. Is there a good place nearby?"

"Yes. Let me just tell Karen we're heading out,

then we can go to Soriano's up the road. It's Mexican, if that's okay with you, and I can be back in an hour."

"Sounds good. I'll drive."

After Samantha informs Frownie Face Karen of our plans (which to my amazement makes her look even more disapproving than her usual at rest face), we head out. Within a few minutes we arrive and are seated in one of the four booths of the quaint Mexican-themed eatery. Samantha has been quiet, only speaking once on the way over to point out that the Genesee County Sheriff's Office is just a block or two down the street from Soriano's. "You can ask for Detective Grant if you want to speak to them about Geoff's case," she informs me.

After placing our orders and starting in on a margarita, I decide I should tell Samantha more if I'm going to get her to open up. "My story involves Geoff and a series of incidents spanning multiple states. He's been linked to young children, toddlers really, whom he has saved from life-threatening situations."

She smiles at this pronouncement. It's a smile that speaks of someone who is thinking fondly of a friend. "That sounds like Geoff. He'd do anything for anyone, especially a child. So, these 'incidents' as you call them, I hope they all had happy endings?"

"Yes. Absolutely. He saved a child in St. Louis from drowning. Saved another in Nashville from heat exhaustion in a locked car. Then he saved a third child just a few weeks ago in Atlanta from poisoning."

Samantha initially seems surprised, but

enthralled by this brief synopsis of events, then the look on her face shows confusion. "Wow! So, wait... that means he's no longer a missing person, right? Oh my God. That is fantastic! I can't wait to tell our colleagues."

"Whoa. Sorry, not so fast. He is still missing, actually. Each time he saved a child, he took off. No one seems to know where he is at the moment. But he's actually missing, times four... four different states; four different missing person cases."

"Oh. So the police are looking for him in all those states?"

"Yes, they are. You see, the thing is, in all of those cases, he disappears before the police can question him about the events. They believe he is a homeless alcoholic, who on three separate occasions has popped up just in the nick of time to save a child. He's used three different aliases before vanishing into thin air. It makes him look suspicious in their eyes."

I can tell I've angered her. "And, what about your eyes, Joanne? Does he look suspicious to you? Of course he does. Why else would you be writing a story about him? It's so typical. The more horrendous the crime, the better the story. Well let me tell you, flat out, if you are looking to bury Geoff you can forget about asking me to help you."

"No, wait. That's not it at all. I have no idea how this story is going to end. But so far, every single person I've interviewed claims he's a hero. But there are never any eyewitnesses who can say beyond a shadow of a doubt what the events were that led up to the child being endangered. The cops want to talk to him. They want to clear him of all suspicion. That's all. And I'd be happy to do the same. I'm not looking to bury anyone, I just want the truth. You have to trust me."

Our food arrives. It gives her pause to think about what I've just told her. "I guess I'm a little protective of Geoff after all that he went through."

"I understand. I really do. Just help me tell his story, that's all I'm asking."

She's very quiet, and I see a tear roll down her face as she reaches into her purse and pulls out a Kleenex. She dabs her eyes. "His story ... it's so sad. I met Geoff about ten years ago. I was the new principal. None of the teachers knew what to expect of me, but I could tell they were not too pleased at my appearance – Powers was a very conservative school. All the staff, except Geoff. He smiled, shook my hand and announced to all of those cynical eyes looking at me, 'Everyone, let's show Samantha some Flint Flyer's spirit. Happy to have you here, Samantha. You are going to love it. Come to our hockey game tonight – our boys will be taking on St. Jude's. It'll be a great chance to rub elbows with the kids, the staff, the parents.' His exuberance was infectious. He broke the ice for me, and really, those doubters had no choice. He was bound and determined to make my time at Powers a success, and more than that, he wanted me to enjoy it too. That was who he was. As a teacher, as a coach, as a family man. He just wanted everyone around him to succeed and be happy." Samantha has regained her composure; just talking about him has made her smile.

"So... what did happen to his family? I've read some newspaper articles, but they're slim on details."

Samantha gathers herself, then starts, "It was the Friday before the Memorial Day long weekend. I ran into Geoff in the staff room. He had been planning to go with his wife Martha and their daughter Jenny back to Martha's hometown, Newberry, where her folks are buried. Her dad was a vet and that town does quite a job with parades and picnics and events like that. Real Americana. They'd planned on camping for the weekend in the Hiawatha National Forest. It's quite the drive from here, over four and a quarter hours.

"Anyway, I asked Geoff if he was looking forward to the weekend, and then I looked at him closely and you could tell he was sicker than a dog. His face was ashen, his hand was trembling a bit, and he seemed pretty weak. I asked him if he was okay, and he said he was. Then he paused and said, 'Actually... I'm not okay... I'm a bit under the weather. Think I may have a touch of the flu.'"

Samantha pauses, then continues, "I guess Martha was really looking forward to the weekend. She hadn't been back home in a few years and had plans to meet up with a couple of her old high school chums. Sort of a small scale class reunion thing. So, anyway, Geoff told me he'd called Martha that afternoon to tell her he wasn't well, and after discussing

212

it, she'd decided she and Jenny would go on without him, and leave him at home to get better. He told me she said something like, 'You can get a lot more rest in an empty quiet house anyway'. I could tell he wasn't too happy about the whole thing. I told him to go home and rest up, that hopefully I'd see him Tuesday after the long weekend if he was feeling better. I guess Martha and Jenny left that afternoon around four o'clock. She'd hoped to get to the campground around nine p.m., set up camp and rest up for Saturday's parade and reunions."

Samantha reaches for her Kleenex and brushes away more tears. "What happened, according to Michigan State Highway Patrol, is that she was cruising on Highway 2, just outside of the little town of Brevort... you know, after you cross the bridge at Machinaw City that separates Lake Michigan from Lake Huron? It's wild country up there. Anyhow, it was pitch dark and, according to the car that was driving behind her, a moose jumped out onto the road from the underbrush, right in front of her. She swerved and hit the brakes hard, but she had no chance in that little car... I think it was a Honda Civic. The car missed the moose, but hit the shoulder and flipped over a couple of times, landing upside down in a deep ditch that runs along the lake side part of the road. They estimated she was doing about sixty miles an hour. According to the autopsy report, Martha was killed instantly. And so was Jenny."

"So, did Geoff tell you all this?"

"Yes, he did. The State troopers broke the news

to him about eleven o'clock that Friday night. Of course, when they do that, they want to make sure that the family member they are breaking the news to is going to be okay. They asked him if there was anyone who could spend the night with him. What they told me is that he just went blank. He couldn't understand, or didn't want to understand, or believe, what they were saying. Then he said he had to see for himself, but the State Troopers told him that wasn't a good idea right then; that he would have to wait until the morning. Then they asked him again who to call. It's so sad. He has no other family and, outside of the school, no close friends. Anyhow, somehow they figured out where he worked and they called me. I hustled over with my husband and we watched over him until about five-thirty Saturday morning. He was still very sick, but he was climbing the walls by then, and he set out for Brevort just as soon as the sun was up. Later that day he called me and confirmed the worst – it was Martha and Jenny... both dead. He could hardly keep it together on the phone."

Taking this all in, I stay quiet as Samantha pauses in her recall and sheds more tears. "I'm so sorry, Samantha, this must be difficult for you. Are you all right?" She nods, then I prompt, "There was no funeral...?"

"No, there wasn't. They were buried in Martha's hometown, Newberry. There was just a graveside service. The funeral home knew Martha's family and made all the arrangements; I don't think

Geoff was in any state of mind to organize anything."

"No, I'm sure he wasn't." I pause to think for a moment. "I didn't come across any newspaper stories about this accident. Do you know why that would be?"

"There was likely an article in the paper but I'm sure they withheld names out of respect for the remaining family, Geoff that is. And because there were no charges laid. " Another mystery solved.

"Did you hear from Geoff after that?"

Samantha takes a deep breath before responding. "Yes, I did. On that Memorial Day Monday, he called me to say he needed some time off before he could come back to work. His plan was to take all the camping things that Martha had packed and stay in the woods for a while by himself. Well, 'a while' turned into three months. I was worried about him, and in August with school about to start in a couple of weeks, I had no choice but to call the sheriff's office up there and see if someone could track him down."

"I take it they found him."

"Yes, they found him. He had checked himself into the Genesee County Mental Health facility. He'd been suffering with severe depression and decided that he needed help. I got a hold of him there, and he insisted that he was feeling more at ease and would be leaving the facility that week. He actually sounded very convincing and I thought that maybe being back at school with the kids and his hockey team would really help him. Then, well, you read the newspaper article... he disappeared. Nobody really knows what happened.

He was here one day and gone the next. I'm guessing he came back to his house, but all those memories of Martha and Jenny just sent him into a spiral. I called the police when he didn't show up for our staff meeting the day before school started and he wasn't answering his phone. I was so worried that he might have done something to himself."

I take this all in. There is one more question I need to ask. "So, this stay in the Genesee County Mental Health facility. That was a one off, right? He didn't otherwise have any history of mental health issues?"

"No, no history of mental health issues whatsoever. And, trust me, I would know. The school board vets our teachers and if there was any mental health issue, I'd know about it."

I've run out of questions and decide to end our meeting. "Well, thank you so much, Samantha. You've really helped fill in some blanks for me. And, you are right... that is a devastatingly sad story. I guess the good news is, we might be able to end on a happier note. As far as we know, he's alive. I promise you if, no, *when* he turns up you will be on my list of people to call."

"Thanks, Joanne. I want him back. The school isn't the same without him. The kids now, none of them would know him. All the students who were here when he was last teaching have now graduated. I can't believe he's been wandering the streets all this time."

We finish our lunch and I drop Samantha back at the school. I'd like one more face-to-face discussion, hopefully today: Detective Grant of the Genesee County Sheriff's office.

I double back to the restaurant, and turn right where Samantha had pointed before lunch. Sure enough, a minute later I'm in the parking lot of the sheriff's department. I don't usually enter a police station without first making an appointment, but I was in the neighborhood and convinced myself that this would be a brief conversation.

I enter the modern building and go through the metal detector. The reception area is light and airy with an abundance of natural light. There is a roped off maze where a few people are waiting to get the attention of one of the three staff sergeants manning the long reception desk. The whole scene reminds me more of a bank than a police station. As I reach the front of the line, the lone female of three desk sergeants catches my eye and asks, "How may I help you?"

"I'd like to speak with Detective Grant, please."

"Okay. Can you sign in on this register first, and produce some ID for me?"

I do as asked, she nods and places a call, asking me as she's dialling, "And what it is you wish to speak with him about?"

"It's about an old missing person case he worked on. Geoffrey Talbot."

After a brief wait, she relays this message, hangs up the phone and directs me. "He'll see you now. Down the hall to the detectives' bullpen on your right.

He'll greet you."

I make my way down the hall, open the door to the 'bullpen' as she called it, and towering just inside the door is the largest black man I've ever seen in my life. "Detective Grant?" I ask, feeling somewhat intimidated by his size.

"Yes. And you are?"

"Joanne Hope. I'm an investigative journalist."

He studies me, and I can see a spark of recognition. "I know you. You're that writer that helped figure out that prostitution ring in Fargo, right?"

"One and the same." He seems pleased that he recalled that detail. I'm equally pleased that he's pleased, because I would not want this man to be unhappy with me.

"Okay, so what brings a Pulitzer nominated writer to this downtrodden place? Sergeant Shelly mentioned something about an old missing person case. You didn't find a bunch of bodies somewhere in Genesee County, I hope."

"No, nothing so dramatic. I did sort of find someone though. Alive. Geoffrey Talbot. He's been missing for over five years."

"Yup, I know that case. So, you found him. Can I ask where, and why you're coming to me if that mystery is solved?"

"Well, knowing he's alive is one thing. Locating him is another."

The detective looks intrigued. He leads me to an interrogation room that looks nothing like the stark concrete ones I've seen recently. It's painted a light green and the chairs are nice faux leather upholstered club chairs. The only thing that gives it away as an interrogation room is the heavy oak table that is bolted to the floor and the strategically placed rings on the table and floor used to secure a prisoner with handcuffs and leg irons if required. I quickly relate the story of Geoffrey's various escapades in St. Louis, Nashville and Atlanta, and explain that he has not actually been located. His eyebrows rise as he quietly digests this information. Then, after a brief pause, he says matter-of-factly, "Well, Ms. Hope, I can see how this story would peak the curiosity of an investigative reporter, but, honestly, we just have a missing person's case. I see nothing more here."

I knew it would be a short conversation, but I wasn't expecting it to be that short. I press on, "So, about his wife and daughter... you knew about all that?"

"Of course. Again though, not relevant to his status as a missing person other than it added to the urgency in finding him. After his stay in the mental health facility, we were concerned he might hurt himself."

"I know I'm going out on a limb here, but did anyone check his alibi, or take a good look at the car his wife Martha was driving at the time of the accident?"

"Okay, I know where you are going with this line of questioning. Trust me, we had a discussion with Mr. Talbot. Of course we had suspicions. You know the usual – husband has an argument with his wife, decides to tamper with his wife's car just before she goes on a nighttime road trip. He conveniently stays home. Then of course, he has conversations and visits with the hot principal at his school."

"I guess I wasn't going that far out on a limb after all."

"No, you weren't. But, the truth is, we had that car forensically examined and found it hadn't been tampered with. And Mr. Talbot, he was not a healthy guy when I interviewed him right after the accident. His alibi was solid. His neighbor talked with him around six-thirty p.m., said he'd arrived home from the drugstore with some flu medications. I actually felt bad for the guy, having to answer our questions. I think it's the reason he ended up in the looney bin. Imagine losing your family and having to go through that type of questioning. When you think about it, maybe that's the reason he keeps moving around. He doesn't want to have anything to do with law enforcement. Can't say I blame him. But we were just doing our job."

"No, I can't say I'd be too anxious to talk to anyone in your line of work after what he'd been through." Questions answered, it's time to wrap it up. "Well, I think that's about it. Thanks for your time, Detective. I can see myself out."

"My pleasure. And listen, if he pops up again, let me know. I'm going to keep the case open in NamUs for now."

"Oh, about that... are you guys the only police force using that database? I have three other forces involved now, and it seems none of them are familiar with it."

"Well, we pride ourselves on being progressive here, Ms. Hope. But, in fairness, it's a pretty new database. Most forces are only now adopting it for use. That said, you may want to encourage your contacts in the other jurisdictions to use it, and to update this case. Multiple sightings should be reported."

"I will do my best, Detective. Not sure it will work, but I can try to encourage them. Thanks again." And with that I depart.

I see no reason to stay in Flint, but the truth is, I'm not sure where to go next. Atlanta is now a dead end. I decide to sleep on it and hopefully come up with an answer in the morning.

Settling into a cheap motel along I-75, I rinse out a pair of socks and undies in the sink and hang them to dry in the shower stall, then order in a pizza from a place recommended by the motel. Mindless television offers a diversion before I turn in for the night. I sleep fitfully as I think of the Professor, or Geoffrey Talbot as I now know him. What a horrible time he must have endured through the summer of 2005. Is it any wonder he decided to drop out of society? I'm not sure how this so far translates into a feature article for Tony and Jerome, so I'm determined to do one more thing before I attempt to write the story. Find him. I don't think he is a mad man who's taking out some kind of twisted revenge on the world, but I won't be sure until I talk to him. And, I'll admit, I'm feeling like this is a guy who needs and deserves someone to take an interest in him.

I awaken early the next morning, and decide to call Captain Freeman in Atlanta to update him on my conversations with Samantha Ing and Detective Grant. I anxiously wait until eight o'clock, and lucky for me, he likes to get to his office early. He lets me ramble on for a few minutes. I think he's enjoying the fact that I'm frustrated. I've hopscotched the country tracking this story and now I'm at an impasse. I'm more desperate now than ever to find our man.

After letting me conclude my exasperated rant with a reminder to him from Detective Grant that Atlanta PD should update the NamUs database, and that St. Louis and Nashville PD's should as well, Freeman says, "Well, thanks for that little lecture on detective procedures, Ms. Hope."

I apologize for my insinuation that his department is incompetent. He accepts my apology, then continues, "Now, I have some news for you. Our guy, who we have now positively ID'd as Geoffrey Talbot, has turned up in Jacksonville, Florida. Imagine that. We managed to find him despite our incompetence."

As I listen with growing excitement, he relates the story of how they found Mr. Talbot.

"Typically, when a missing person case is created all the local police forces (and sometimes state forces) as well as hospitals are notified. The opposite is also true. If someone comes into a hospital emergency ward with something, but without ID and without the assistance of a friend or relative, the admittance area will check to see if they can find a match between the missing persons reports and the patient's appearance. Weather a match is found or not, they contact the local PD. In Talbot's case, he ended up at Baptist Medical Center in Jacksonville a few days ago after a brush with some bad meth. According to the staff there he got lucky – he was very close to dying when he was admitted. But there was no Florida missing person record for a man of his description at the time of admittance, so no luck there. Anyhow, they fixed him up and held him for the mandatory forty-eight hours, then released him.

Here's where our luck comes into it. Apparently a hospital orderly had played high school hockey in Flint a few years back, and he thought the unidentified, homeless OD looked like rival school's coach, Mr. Talbot, only now quite a bit rougher. He asked the patient if he was Coach Talbot, who mumbled something like, 'Once upon a time. Here from Atlanta.' The orderly had the smarts to inform the doctor, who called Jacksonville PD, who called me. We connected the dots between the missing person report and the unidentified patient. Unfortunately, they'd already released him before someone could catch up with him."

"Wow. Do Dunn and Marvel know yet?"

"Yes. We've had a discussion. So, here's how we're going to play it. I've asked Jacksonville PD to try and keep tabs on him. They've seen him around, and apparently keeping tabs won't be too difficult as he has a habit of visiting his local booze store near the Baptist Medical Centre on a daily basis, then sleeping it off on a park bench or under the I-95 bridge. His world is very small. Once our little posse arrives in Jacksonville, they'll bring him in for an interview."

I remind Freeman that I'm supposed to be a member of his so-called posse. I can almost picture him shrugging. I'm a member of the posse, but I don't have a horse, so if I fall behind, that's too bad.

"Ms. Hope, after what you've told me I doubt there will be much to question him about. We think he's a harm only to himself but we would like to identify him and close these missing person cases. But, don't worry, we won't snatch him and release him before you get your face-to-face time with him. When can you get to Jacksonville?"

"I can get there today. I'm sure there are flights from Detroit."

"Okay. We'll be right behind you. We can ask Jacksonville PD to pick him up tomorrow morning."

"Great. See you there."

We end the call. I'm giddy. After so many weeks of hoping to speak with this elusive man, I'm finally going to get my chance.

I call Jerome and he conferences Tony in on the call. I explain that things are moving quickly, but it seems not fast enough for Tony. "Joanne, you have only ninety-six hours... that's four days... to submit what I hope will be a well-polished article. I won't have time to edit the thing if we have any hope to make our deadline." I inwardly groan, and roll my eyes. Tony hasn't edited my work in a long time. But I don't give him the gears. Instead I just reiterate my best intentions to finish the story on time.

Jerome adds, "Well, it sounds like you've really worked all the angles on this, Joanne. I look forward to reading your piece." His voice seems to have an edge, but I know he's still got my back. I pack my carry-on. It's time to head back to Detroit, return the rental Equinox and catch a flight to sunny Florida. I won't miss Michigan.

Jacksonville, February 2010

I book a non-stop Delta flight from Detroit to Jacksonville, which, including ground time will only take four hours. I've got a head start on Dunn, Marvel, Freeman, and the Jacksonville PD. They want to pick him up tomorrow for their interrogation; but I have other plans.

What I have gathered from my call with Freeman is that Geoffrey Talbot is a man of habits. He frequents an alcohol store near Baptist Medical Center on a daily basis, and doesn't stray too far from that area. My plan is simple. I'm going to rent a car, then I'm going to scour the area around the medical center for booze outlets. When I spot a likely location, I'll ask whoever is manning the till if they've seen Geoffrey, aka 'the Professor'. I still have a photo that should help in that regard. If I'm in any luck he won't have made his daily purchase yet, so I can stake out the joint (as the cops would say) and hope to spot him and talk to him before the Jacksonville PD makes their move.

I'm through the Avis checkout, armed with an Atlas map of the city. Today must be my lucky day. The Baptist Medical Center is only a twenty minute drive straight down I-95, and I arrive there around two p.m. Usually the hectic pace I set for myself starting early this morning would have drained me by now and I'd be looking forward to checking into a nice hotel and flopping on the bed to catch a nap before cocktail hour.

But, my adrenaline level today is high. I'm certain I'm on the right path. I pull into a parking spot and take a closer look at the map. The medical center is essentially on a peninsula surrounded by the St. John River on three sides. There isn't much of anything east of the interstate, and the river is north of the hospital, so that narrows my search considerably to just the several blocks south of the hospital and between the interstate and the west bank of the peninsula. I pull out of the parking spot and head south on San Marco Boulevard, a major artery. Within minutes, I spot an enormous neon sign, 'Big Al's Liquor Outlet'. I can't contain my excitement. Could this be it? What are the odds?

I find parking in the rear of the building, and make my way to the front, where I can see the posted hours as twelve noon until ten p.m., Monday to Saturday. Thankfully today isn't Sunday. I enter the store and am greeted with the lecherous stare of a man in his mid-fifties who looks to be roughly five eight, and two hundred and eighty pounds. His gut hangs over his belt and stretches his stained white tee shirt to the breaking point. "Can I help you, ma'am?" he asks, with a southern drawl and leering eyes.

I decide I will purchase a bottle of nice white wine to help encourage conversation, and hopefully move his eyes away from my chest. "I think I can find what I'm looking for, but thanks." I make my way down the aisle toward the sign labelled 'fine wines' and select an expensive bottle of Sauvignon Blanc from the Marlborough region of New Zealand. I've found that the more money I throw around, the more talkative people are likely to be.

I make my way to the checkout, where Mr. Lecherous smiles showing off his yellow stained teeth, and says "Now that there's a very fine white. I think y'all will enjoy it. Special occasion?"

"No, not really. I'm just in town for the evening and thought I'd treat myself to some nice wine. I'll get some less expensive take-out to go with it." Ice broken, I start my probe. "I'm in town hoping to track down my poor brother. He's had a bit of breakdown and the last thing he said before he left Michigan was that he needed to get down to Jacksonville where we used to go on our family vacations, to get warm and get his head together. I'm worried about him. He's done this kind of thing before, and it usually ends up with him in rehab."

"Really. Now that's a shame. He's lucky to have a sister like you to look out for him."

"That's kind of you to say. By the way, he loves this part of the city, especially loves the river. Maybe he's even been in this store, given he's likely off the wagon."

"Maybe. Do ya' have a picture?"

"Sure. Here's a photo, taken a year or so ago. He's 38 years old, average build and height. Does he look familiar?"

"That guy? That guy is your brother? Lady, y'all have come to the right place, and judging by his recent behaviour, youse lucky youse tracked him down. He's been on an epic binge for quite some time. Comes in here every day and buys a jug of the hard stuff."

"Oh, my God. Are you serious!?" I can barely contain my excitement. This must be my lucky day. "Has he come in yet today?"

"No, but he usually comes in around between noon and four... I guess happy hour is important to him." He chuckles, like he finds 'my brother's' addiction somehow amusing. I let it slide.

"Well, I can't thank you enough. I'll just wait around outside and hope that he shows up."

"Well, miss, we can do better than that. If you like, y'all can wait in my back office, maybe we can get to know each other a little bit. How's about we open one of those fine bottles of wine? On the house."

I can barely conceal my disgust. But I've come this far, and don't want to endanger my plan. In case Geoffrey doesn't show up today, I need Prince Charming on my side. If he tries something, I'm confident I can look after myself. "All right, that sounds lovely. You really are a gentleman helping a damsel in distress, aren't you?"

He gives that same little chuckle and I can see his eyes are dancing with undisguised glee as he shuffles to the front door. I notice he flips a sign hanging on the door. He catches the look on my face and says, "Oh, that just says 'back in 15.' I'd like to have a bite to eat while we have a drink, if you don't mind. I often take a break around this time of day."

"Of course. I don't mind at all."

"Right this way, my dear," he instructs me, then shuffles down the aisle and selects a bottle of the same Sauvignon Blanc I just bought. I follow him back into his office.

The long narrow office is dimly lit, but as my eyes adjust I take in the details. There are a couple of metallic filing cabinets against a greyish green wall that is dominated by a poster of 'Dogs Playing Poker.' Across from the cabinets in the narrow eight foot space, is a worn leather sofa with a dingy stained comforter which has clearly seen better days. At the back of the office, several feet past the end of the sofa, is an old oak desk, with a desk lamp and a fan perched on opposing corners. The desk is strewn with papers. A back door is just to the left of the desk and I see it's dead-bolted. I feel slightly uneasy but know I have to keep on this guy's good side.

"Tell me, Miss... uh... oh, I didn't catch your name," he says, as he scrutinizes the top of the bottle, presumably to see if he's in luck and it's a screw top. It is.

"It's Hope. Joanne Hope."

"Now that's a pretty name. Where there's hope there's a way ... isn't that what they say? You can call me Will, short for William."

"I'd never heard that saying before, Will. In fact I thought it was 'where there is a will there is a way'."

He laughs open-mouthed like a hyena, as if I have just said the funniest thing he's ever heard. "My, my. Isn't that funny. I'm 'Will'... you're 'Hope' –

together we should find a way." He grins and shakes his head in amusement.

I politely laugh at his stupid play on words. He pours us both a glass of wine. I use the word glass generically. His wine is in a coffee mug, mine is in a disposable take-out cup. Classy. He saunters over and closes the office door. He's now creeping me out, and I'm really regretting accepting his invitation to stick around here. I stand as close to the office door as I can, planning a quick exit just in case.

He moves to the sofa and pats the seat beside him. "Come here pretty lady, take a load off."

"Oh, no, I really shouldn't. You go ahead and eat your lunch now, I'll just wait here."

"No, I insist. You come sit here where it's comfy, and let's get to know each other better."

My stomach is starting to churn. I've always prided myself on being able to read a situation. It's a tool I've honed over the years as an investigative journalist. You take calculated risks to try to get your story. Now, the realization starts to sink in that I might have taken too big a risk. My mind is racing, thinking of how to quickly extricate myself from this situation. I pretend to take a sip of my wine, then look at my watch and exclaim, "Oh my goodness! Where has the time gone? I just lost track. I really need to leave right now to check into my hotel before they think I've cancelled and give my room away."

I start to reach for the door handle, and suddenly, the man calling himself 'Will', fat as he is, moves with the speed of a gazelle, blocking my path.

His grin has disappeared and his face has turned mean. "Now, that's not very nice. I go to the trouble of opening a thirty dollar bottle of wine, and you can't even do me the courtesy of showing some gratitude. No, Miss Hope, we're going have some fun, you and me."

He grabs my wrist and with an effortless push, sends me sprawling onto the sofa. My mind does a cartwheel. I realize how foolish I've been, and the price I might end up paying. Before I can right myself, he's on top of me... all two hundred and eighty sweaty pounds.

"Get off of me! Get off of me!" I scream, as I kick out, and try to free my hands to gouge his eyes.

His shoulders have me pinned. His breath smells like decay as his coarse voice (not the melodious southern drawl of our earlier conversation) berates me, "You slut. You think you don't owe me? I'll bet you're like your brother.... just a piece of white trash. Haven't worked a day in your life, but you want the best wine. Just like him, a disrespectful drunk, coming in here every day buying the best booze I got. You, putting on your airs. Well, I'm as good as you are, I'm better in fact. Where does a homeless guy get that kind of money? He's probably like you, giving blow jobs to anyone willing to pay. Well, you're gonna' pay for that wine I just opened... you can count on that."

I scream again, and he leans back and backhands me. Hard. I'm seeing stars. I keep screaming and swearing as loud as I can, twisting and bucking to try and get him off of me. He shouts at me to shut up as he rips at my silk shirt and I hear buttons fly across the floor. My head is spinning as I try to raise my hands and claw at his face, but he still has me pinned. He just weighs too much. I struggle but I just can't move. He leans back and punches me, once, twice. I feel like I'm about to black out as I see him slowly rise from the sofa and then his pants drop to his ankles.

And that's when it happens. The office door flies open and my assailant is suddenly sent careening the length of the office, his head thudding against the oak desk. He staggers up, turns back to face his assailant, and is greeted with a hard left jab to the face, followed by a devastating round house right that sends him reeling and renders him unconscious. This entire episode lasts less than ten seconds. I'm recovering from my own beating, so it doesn't register right away. When the adrenaline rush has subsided ever so slightly, and I'm able to focus on my knight in shining armour, I'm astounded by what I see. Without thinking and purely driven by overwhelming relief and excitement, I blurt out, "Geoffrey... Geoffrey Talbot... you're here. You saved me from that disgusting piece of shit..."

_____

_____

I slept later than I intended. Of course, it could have been the jug of Jack Daniel's and the late night (early morning?) beer chasers that caused my lethargy. Either way, I'm parched, my hands are shaking and I've got nothing to drink. I pull myself off my pallet bed, and stumble down to the river. The ear splitting sound of some asshole on a jet ski showing off for his bikini-clad girlfriend who's perched on the opposite shore is enough to make me vomit, which I do, much to the chagrin of the asshole and his girlfriend. I dip my head in the river water several times to clear my head, to shouts of 'loser' and 'jerkoff' from the yuppie on the jet ski. After giving him the finger and a few choice invectives of my own, I wander back through the underbrush to my bed and light up a reefer. I glance at the sun and figure it must be nearing two p.m. I really did sleep in.

The slight buzz I've got going counteracts the headache that's starting to pound my dusty cranium. I need to get to my cash stash and buy a bottle while I'm still slightly stoned/drunk, or run the risk of a nasty hangover. I wander past the medical center, over to Treaty Oak Park, grab a few twenties, and double back towards Big Al's. The morning is pleasantly warm with a mild breeze... perfect day for a little stroll. Sometimes, when it's like this and the city streets are quiet, I think to myself that maybe my plan to slowly drink myself to death is really paying dividends. After all, if I had killed myself quickly, say, five years ago, I would have missed out on times like these. At least this way, I can still enjoy the occasional minute or two of beauty and tranquility before I cash in my chips. It dawns on me, in my semi-buzzed state, just how ludicrous this thought is; how contradictory. Anyhow, enough deep thoughts. That only leads to dark thoughts. Time to get shit-faced.

I arrive at Big Al's and, much to my annoyance, the sign on the door reads 'Back in 15'. In my many visits to the fat man's establishment, I've never once seen that sign. Usually, the fat bastard is perched on his stool by the cash register and sneers at me through the window, before I even crack the door open. I stand at the door, dumbfounded. Fat Al is nowhere in sight. Maybe fifteen minutes isn't really fifteen minutes... maybe he's just taking a quick bio break, I think. But I can't stand here waiting for fifteen minutes... I just can't. I eye the merchandise through the window. I try the door handle, and much to my delight, it's not locked. This helps reinforce my theory that Fat Al is just relieving himself. "Fuck it... I'm thirsty...I'm going in," I say aloud, to no one, and enter the store.

As I'm making my way towards the whiskey section I hear a loud thud from the back of the store, then a female voice shouting, 'Get off of me!', then more loud thumps and some very loud swearing and shrieking. I quickly head towards the noise and hear more commotion coming from behind a closed door marked 'Staff Only.' From the sounds I know something nasty is going on in there, and I smash the door open. That's when I see them – her, lying on the sofa with her eyelids drooping and her eyes rolling back in her head – and him, standing over her, yanking his pants down.

I grab the fat son of a bitch, and spin him around. He staggers with his pants around his ankles and I see his eyes bulge in astonishment, as I use his off balance momentum to hurtle him across the room into the office desk. He's dazed as he gets up from the floor, and I can see that a look of pure white hot hate has replaced the look of astonishment on his face. Before he has time to gather his wits, I rear back and throw a left jab followed by a right handed hay maker. My hockey days taught me a few boxing lessons. I hear his nose shatter and watch as he staggers backwards. He slumps and sinks down, out cold. My right hand throbs, but it's not a feeling I'm unfamiliar with.

The woman, still sprawled on the sofa and just starting to comprehend what's happened, is squinting up at me. Then I hear something that doesn't register at first. My name. My real name, "Geoffrey Talbot."

She says it again, and adds, "You saved me from that disgusting piece of shit."

At that point she briefly loses consciousness and I shake her gently to rouse her. "Lady, lady, wake up!" I see a disposable cup holding some kind of clear beverage and, hoping it contains cold water, splash a bit over her face. It's wine, but it seems to do the trick as she then wakens with a groggy, "What the hell? Geoffrey Talbot?"

The adrenaline rush has overcome both my buzz and my headache, and I'm now totally flabbergasted. "How... how do you know my name?"

"It's a long story." Her words are slurred, and I know it's not from the wine... that fat asshole has done a number on her face.

"I haven't heard someone use my real name in over five years."

"Yeah. You look like you've just seen a ghost." She modestly closes her blouse, and gingerly rises to a sitting position on the sofa.

"Well, metaphorically, I have. That guy, Geoff, he doesn't exist anymore. This guy, this hungover and very thirsty guy, he's taken his place. Now, if you'll excuse me, I don't much care to be around when fat boy over there regains consciousness. I don't think you need me any further, so I'll just grab some essentials and be on my way." I want to put as much space between me and this situation as I can, and fast.

"Wait. Please don't leave without me. I need to talk to you – to tell you some things... and I need for you to tell me some things."

"Look, lady, I don't know who you are, and if you want to talk I guess that's okay. But I'm afraid if you want to press charges against this piece of shit you're on your own – I've got to get out of here. The last thing I need is to be here when Big Al wakes up. He's likely to call the cops, or worse, he's likely to go behind that cash register and pull out that hand gun he keeps under the counter."

"He'd be awfully stupid to call the cops, seeing as how he'd be charged with assault and attempted rape. But I don't want to go that route either, and I certainly don't enjoy the thought of that piece of garbage pointing a gun at us. Let's go. And, I have a bottle of wine that I already paid for, so hopefully that will suffice for now." I think the wine offer tipped the scales for me.

"For now. OK, let's go."

"I have a rental car out back. Let's go for a drive."

I grab a jacket to hide my ripped blouse, and use some bottled water and a tee shirt to wash my face. Geoff climbs into the passenger seat, opens the proffered bottle of wine and downs half of it without taking a breath. He wasn't kidding when he said he was thirsty.

He starts, "All right, you said you had some things you wanted to tell me."

"Yes, and I want you to tell me a few things, too."

We are driving on the I-95, heading south. When I cooked up this plan, I had intended to stay in Jacksonville, have my chat with the elusive Mr. Talbot, then lead the police to where they could find him. Now, things are different, and I'm not sure what my next move should be. Everything has happened so fast. So, driving buys me time. It also buys him time, and I think when he hears what I have to say, he's going to want to take it.

So I begin. "Okay, well, where to start? Do the names Gordon Howe, Brett Hull and David Legwand mean anything to you? Or, how about 'the Professor'?"

I glance over at him. He's got a funny look on his face, like he's unsure what to think. Then, much to my surprise, he laughs. Not a full belly laugh. More like an ironic laugh.

"Well, you really are quite clever, aren't you? Tell me, Ms. uhh…"

"Hope… Joanne Hope." I fill in the blank for him.

"Okay, Joanne Hope, tell me, why are you so interested in me and what I did back in St. Louis, Nashville and Atlanta?"

Now it's my turn to laugh. "Are you serious? You saved three children from life threatening situations. Don't you think that's reason enough for someone to be interested in you? Especially if that someone is an investigative reporter?"

"Oh, so that's the deal. Well that's good, because I thought you might be law enforcement. I should have guessed you aren't, given how you put yourself in danger with Fat Al. What were you thinking, anyway?"

In all the excitement, I've forgotten to express my appreciation to him for getting me out of trouble. "About that. Thank you. I owe you big time. I guess you've now notched another good deed. And on that note… you mentioned law enforcement. Are you aware that you are now the subject of 'missing person' cases spanning four different states? And, here's where it's kind of tricky, three of those states are teetering on

239

linking your missing person case to a child endangerment case. That's one of the reasons I went looking for you. I want to hear your side of the story before law enforcement does."

"Whoa. That's a lot to take in." He pauses for a moment as he wraps his mind around it. "First, you're welcome. Second, I'm not surprised I've created a wake of missing person cases. Third... child endangerment? Well... again I shouldn't be surprised, but still, what the fuck? Why is it that people automatically want to think the worst? I wasn't looking for any of this. Those incidents just happened. And I don't regret that I was able to save those little kids. Not a bit. But damn it! Just like I knew it would.... it's happening again...!" His voice is now quivering with rage, and something else. There is a deep sense of melancholy.

He turns to face the passenger window, but I can see he's trying really hard not to cry. In fact, he isn't succeeding. A tear rolls down his face. I reach over, pat his arm and hand him a Kleenex. He's not at all embarrassed. He actually seems more detached than embarrassed. As I think back to my discussion with Detective Grant in Flint Michigan, I think I know what's happening. He's reliving the questioning about the death of his wife and child. I need to get him back to the present.

"Hey, Geoffrey, I understand. I really do. I talked to Detective Grant in Flint. I know what happened to your wife and daughter, and I know he asked you some pretty shitty questions about that. It is no wonder that you're not too fond of speaking with law enforcement, or for that matter even speaking with me."

He swivels in his seat to face me. "And what about you? Investigative Reporter. Do you think I wore a cape and tights? That I was some kind of real life super hero, rescuing kids? Or do you think I'm a creep, out on some sick spree? You know, I'd bet on the latter. After all, who wants to read good news? Just like the police. Asking me over and over again if I killed my family. I bet your editor is going ape shit thinking about how much revenue he can generate with an exclusive story about the murderer and child molester posing as a hero, right? I'll tell you why I'm running. I'm running because I can't trust anyone. And I'm running because I need to drink. Uninterrupted. Until I drop dead. That's my very simple plan. Now, if you'd be so kind, I want out. Next interchange."

I have to think fast. How do I keep him from running again? Maybe, just maybe, the truth will put us back on course. "I'm going to level with you, Geoff. The truth is, when I first started to put the pieces together, I did think there was a possibility that you were up to no good. I mean, what are the odds of being in the right place at the right time on three separate occasions? I'd venture pretty slim. And, you doing a disappearing act after each encounter did make you look suspicious. But, then I started to talk to everyone. Parents and guardians like Elmira in St. Louis, and Annette in Atlanta. Even just acquaintances like your

241

friend Joey in St. Louis, Martin in Nashville and Damon and Doris in Atlanta. Not a soul amongst them believed for a minute you could harm anyone. Just the opposite. They do think you wear a cape and tights. And I talked to your former principal... Samantha. She told me how hurt you were, and how worried they all are, still to this day, back in Flint. She also told me that they need you, back at your job. You know, you don't have to do this to yourself. There is now no doubt in my mind that you saved those children. As for law enforcement, I've been in touch with all of them. Sure, they had suspicions, but in every case, they have zero evidence that you did anything wrong. More than anything, they just want to close their cases and confirm what we just talked about, without any FBI involvement. You're a hero, not a creep or a criminal."

He pauses. I can see the wheels spinning. He takes another long haul of wine. "Okay... I believe you. I believe you talked to all those people, and that you know I'm not some sick pervert. I'm still not sure about the cops... but I'm tired of running. Are you able to help me clear this up with them, so I can be left alone to drink in peace?"

I nod in agreement. "Absolutely, I can. I will. I've been told by one of them that representatives from all three forces, St. Louis, Nashville and Atlanta, will rendezvous tomorrow here in Jacksonville for a discussion with you."

"Oh, so my days are numbered anyhow. Looks like the gum shoes are hot on my trail."

"Yes, they are. That's why I wanted to get to you first. I didn't want you to get spooked and run again, and I wanted to give you a chance to tell your story."

"Well, it sounds like you pretty much know my story."

"I do and I don't. Look, can we maybe stop somewhere? I'll buy you dinner and all you can drink. What do you say?"

"Well, I've got a busy day of nothing scheduled, but, how can I refuse an offer like that?"

We continue on I-95 for another hour. The travel time seems to take the edge off everything. Geoff relaxes as he finishes the bottle of wine. My mind wanders while I'm at the wheel. Maybe I'll have nightmares about Fat Al in the days to come, but right now I'm feeling pretty relaxed. I spot a billboard advertising 'St. Mary's Seafood and More' at the next exit. I get Geoff's attention and nod towards the billboard, "What do you think? Do you like seafood?"

"Sure, I like seafood. I just hope the 'and More' means booze."

"I promised you all you could drink, and I will deliver on that promise."

"Okay, let's stop there then. I'm starting to get the shakes."

We find the place, just off International Golf Parkway, and head inside. On entry there is a sign advertising that today is 'Martini Thursday'. Martinis for four dollars. I'm a bit concerned that Geoff might be

243

an incoherent drunk by the time we order dinner, but, a promise is a promise. The interior is a bit dated, but clean and airy. I notice there is large deck out back that overlooks a small pond. It's set up for diners, and it's deserted. "Do you mind eating outside? The weather here is so nice after my trip to Flint. And I don't want to scare anyone with my messed up face."

We're seated outside and order a round of vodka martinis. I look at Geoff and decide this tranquil setting is as good an opportunity as any to get to know him.

"So, our deal included you filling me in on your story. But look, I don't want you to feel like I've somehow maneuvered you into this. If you want to call off the whole thing, I can just drive you to the next town and you can be on your merry way. I won't tell law enforcement about any of this."

"No, that's fine. The truth is these martinis are too good to pass up. And I guess I could use someone to talk to."

Our martinis are already empty – I guess we were both thirsty. He orders another one. I have soda water. "All right then, let's start at the beginning. Tell me about meeting Martha and starting your family."

"Okay. Well... we met at the University of North Dakota. I was a foreign student on a hockey scholarship, fresh off the bus from my home town... that would be Port Hope, Ontario, Canada... and I was really lost on campus. Just basically in awe of the whole thing. I'm wandering through the quad, lugging my backpack and hockey gear around, trying to figure out where my dorm is. I must have looked like a complete hay seed. Anyhow, just as I'm starting to think I've made a huge mistake going to UND instead of playing junior hockey back home, I get this tap on the shoulder. I turn around, and I'm greeted with this vision of loveliness. Just this stunning creature. Blonde, blue eyed, full figured Viking Goddess." He smiles at the memory and continues, "Martha introduces herself and welcomes me to UND frosh week, asks me if she can help me with my stuff. I can't believe my luck. She's second year and on the welcome committee. I mean of all the luck, I stumble onto her my first day there. Anyhow, she helps me locate my dorm, which takes about fifteen minutes. It's a pretty expansive campus, but I'm happy about that, because it gives me time to get to know her. She's doing a bachelor program in social work – that's her all over. She always wanted to help other people. I told her I was doing a business degree, but my real love was hockey and my ambition was to one day play in the NHL. She was impressed. Turns out she was a puck head, just like me. We really hit it off. So... when we get to my room I just blurt out 'Let me buy you dinner... to thank you for your help.' That was our first date, and from that day on we were just about inseparable."

"So, college sweethearts. That's so wonderful. Go on... I'm all ears."

"No. More than just college sweethearts. We were there for each other. And believe me when I tell you this... without Martha, my life would have been over long ago." He's quiet for a moment and then continues. "I had a pretty good rookie season playing UND hockey, and in my second year I was actually selected by the Toronto Maple Leafs in the fourth round of the NHL draft. I was feeling pretty good about myself. And Martha... well, she's just over the moon proud of me. Anyhow, I go to my first pro training camp that fall, and I blow out my left knee. I mean, just destroy it. My NHL dream is done. I'm devastated. I'd dreamt of it my entire life, and it's over just like that." He snaps his fingers for emphasis, his brow furrows as he relives the memory.

"I was depressed and started to drink, smoke a lot of pot. After a month of me moping around and making some very lame attempts at rehabbing my knee, Martha snapped. She just laid into me. 'What kind of man are you? You have one setback, and now you're starting to turn into a complete loser. Skipping classes. Missing rehab for your knee. Getting drunk or stoned every night.' Then she said, 'Shape the fuck up mister, or we're done'."

"Tough love. You know... that can sometimes backfire." My own past briefly comes into my thoughts.

"I sure know that. At first it almost did. I was dumbfounded. I started to literally shake with anger. But... thank God... I didn't say or do anything stupid, I just walked away, went for a long walk around campus. After I calmed down I spent a few hours doing some serious soul searching, and it finally dawned on me that she was right. I was being a little baby. It was time to face my future like an adult. So, I apologized to her for how I'd been acting. I was ashamed and told her she was right. I told her I'd do anything to win back her respect. I actually broke down in tears. Then she started to cry and she told me that we could do this together. That together we could get me back on track. And, no, she didn't want to lose me. She had to muster a lot of courage to confront me like that."

I look at him across the table and I can see that again, he's transported back to that conversation. The start of a tear forms in the corner of his eyes. I order him another martini as our food orders arrive. I've got seabass in white wine sauce with a side of fries and coleslaw. He's having some braised scallops with linguini and pesto. The interruption is welcome; it helps him regain his train of thought and also leads to my next question. "So, you had Martha to help you through that tough time. Anyone else? Family? Friends?"

"No, not really. My parents passed away when I was fourteen, and I was an only child. No aunts, uncles or grandparents either. I ended up as a foster kid for a couple of years, then I spent time with billets when I was playing midget hockey in Toronto. I didn't have much of a life outside of hockey in those days. My teammates were my real family, but, you know... people move on. Most of those guys either went on to other university programs in the US or Canada, or played junior in the Canadian Hockey League."

"So, what about Martha? What about her family?"

"Her mom had passed away when she was in her junior year in high school. And, like me, she was an only child. So it was just her and her dad living in a little town called Newberry, in north Michigan. And her dad, well, they'd never really been close. When her mom passed she said her dad just retreated further into his own little world. And most of her friends just shied away from her after that. They seemed embarrassed, or didn't know what to say. She couldn't wait to leave town and start over at UND. In her first year, she said she made a couple of friends in her dorm, but they dropped out after their first year."

"Then you found each other... two lost and lonely souls."

"Well, I wouldn't be that dramatic about it, but yeah, that's about it."

"Tell me about your marriage."

"Martha finished her undergrad at UND. She told me she was thinking of doing a doctorate program. Her dad had passed away the previous year; there was no reason for her to go back to Newberry, plus he had left her some money from the sale of the family home. Anyhow, I had the feeling she was sticking around because of me, to see me through my last year. I told her that, kind of in jest, and she just stared at me, then got a look like she was about to cry. That's when I knew for sure. I just said to her, 'Martha, marry me. Let's have a life together.' She said, 'It's about time, you jerk.' We both laughed so hard... anyhow, we got married after I graduated.

"At first, we didn't have a pot to piss in. Martha had a part time job working with a drug abuse program in Fargo and it was pretty bleak. She'd come home an emotional wreck on the days she worked. And, I can tell you from my recent life on the streets, I can understand why. Anyhow, her job wasn't paying much. I'd switched from business to the education program in my second year, so when I graduated I got on the list for substitute teachers. I was getting the occasional call to fill in. It was hard to make ends meet, but we were happy.   I was sending out resumes to different school boards in Michigan, the Dakotas, and Wisconsin, figuring I could teach and maybe get into coaching; those states are all hockey hotbeds. Then I got a call from Powers Catholic High. I'd heard about the school. It's a hockey powerhouse in Flint and the surrounding area. Martha was almost as happy as I was when I told her about the opportunity. I got the job and we relocated in time for the school year... it was September, 2000.

"Martha landed a part time job at a non-profit, helping out at a youth shelter. I was teaching and was the assistant coach that first year with the Flint Flyers. Then when Sam Trent, who was the head coach, retired, he recommended me for the job. We moved out of the little apartment we had rented to a two bedroom bungalow that was walking distance to the school. So, you know, everything was really happening for us. We were so incredibly happy."

"It sounds like you had a lovely life with Martha. When did your daughter make her appearance?"

"Well, one day, I came home from school... it was early October 2002. I remember like it was yesterday. When I opened the door, I could smell fresh paint. Martha was nowhere to be seen, but I could hear music coming from the den, at the back of the house. I made my way back, and there she is, in her coveralls, her hair up in a pony-tail, barefoot, up on a ladder, singing away to some Billy Joel tune. She'd pushed all the furniture to one side of the room and had painted two of the walls a pale pink. She didn't even notice me come in. I cleared my throat, and she turned around and smiled, and asked me how I liked it. I laughed and said, 'Well, it's different. When my players come for meetings I'm sure it will elicit some comments.' And she says, 'I don't think you'll be meeting players in this room anymore.' And that's when it hit me. She's pregnant! Before I can say a word, she just gets off the ladder and literally runs to me across the room and jumps into my arms. 'How far along?' I ask, and she says, 'I think about two months.' I asked her how she knows it's a girl and she says she's pretty sure. Then she laughed and said she hadn't seen a doctor, but she just knew – she knew she was pregnant and she knew she was going to have a girl. And, of course, she was right. Jenny was born in June 2003."

Then Geoff breaks down. It's hard to witness. Between sobs he relates how beautiful and smart his little girl was. How she completed their little family. How happy they were.

"Geoff, we can stop here if you like. I'm sure this isn't easy for you."

"No, that's all right. You know something? You're the first person I've actually talked to about any of this in quite some time; well, really... ever."

"Really?? I mean... sorry... I don't mean to sound so incredulous. It's just that, well, you spent several months in a mental health facility. Didn't they provide any grief counselling?"

"Not really. They just medicated me, for the most part."

"Tell me about your time away from Flint, afterwards... in Newberry. What happened? The obit was so brief, so impersonal. I thought it seemed strange."

"I know that now. At the time, I just wasn't functioning. I got to Martha's home town and there were a few people offering condolences, but it got to me, especially after the way some of those people had treated Martha after her mother's death. Really, only her childhood friends Judy and Kate truly cared. I told the funeral home to publish a notice in the paper.

"I was questioned by the police. If you believe it, they thought I had something to do with their deaths. They said they knew about the argument that I had with Martha before she left. Can you imagine how that made me feel? Like I needed reminding... It was just too much. All I wanted to do was get the hell out of Dodge at that point. After the graveside service I beat it into the bush."

"Samantha told me as much. Did you really plan on spending three months in the wilderness? Tell me what happened out there."

"In answer to your question, no, not really. I just needed to get away some place quiet and it seemed like a good idea. But, in hindsight, maybe it wasn't such a great idea. Maybe I should have returned to Flint. Being around Samantha and her husband Mark and some of the other staff members from the school might have prevented what happened next."

"What did happen next?"

"I find this really hard to describe, mainly because I really wasn't all together lucid. The first couple of weeks I was out there I spent a lot of time hiking and just sitting and staring at the campfire. I barely ate or slept. Then, I started to have these visions. Some of them beautiful – euphoric even – of Martha and Jenny. I'd see them in the woods, picking wild flowers... Jenny giggling, Martha singing some song from one of Jenny's Disney movies. I'd try to join them, but then they'd just disappear. So, I learned not to do that, I'd just watch them from afar. I mean, it seemed so real. Then, other times – the bad times – I'd see them, but instead of being happy and picking wild flowers in a forest glen, they'd be... well... they'd be dead."

He breaks down again. I rub his arm to comfort him. He's gasping for air, and trying hard to pull himself together. When he can finally speak again, he continues with his story.

"Anyhow... this goes on for weeks, months... I don't know, I kind of lost track of time. Then one day I'm watching Martha and Jenny, it's a happy one, and Martha turns and looks right at me and for the first time she speaks to me. She says, 'I love you, Geoff, but you need to get some help. Right now. Get out of these woods before it's too late.' I nod and say, something like, 'Okay, Martha, I will... I love you too', then she and Jenny disappear into thin air.

"Then, I do as I'm told. I literally sprinted back to my campsite, packed up my gear and made a beeline to the Genesee County Mental Health facility, which was fairly close to our home in Flint and was the only place I could think of that might be able to help."

"So, you spent, what, a couple of months there?"

"Yes. When I arrived I told them my story. A shrink I spoke to told me that I was suffering from acute depression and anxiety, brought on by the deaths of my loved ones and worsened by inadequate food and sleep, and dehydration. He prescribed some medication that he said would counter the chemical imbalance and bring me back to 'equilibrium', and would allow me to eat and sleep again."

"And... I guess it sort of worked...?"

"The thing is, yes, after a couple of weeks on the meds, I stopped hallucinating and did regain a bit of my appetite. I slept fitfully, but enough. I think they were successful in treating the anxiety, but, the depression, well... that's another story. It seemed the more I regained control of my thoughts, the more they kept returning to the realization that I'd never see my family again. I had checked myself in to the facility, so I had every right to check myself out. I started to think of checking myself out... and then really checking out, if you follow me."

"Suicide."

"Yes. Anyhow, I went home to Flint, and Samantha and her husband and a couple other faculty members came over to express their condolences, and to ask me if I needed anything. You know... awkward for them and me... but they meant well. I shuffled around the house, not knowing what to do with myself, going through periods of depression where I'd hold a gun to my head but then I'd stop short of pulling the trigger. I started to drink at nights. Pretty hard. I'd black out. Then nights turned into days; I'd just drink round the clock to numb myself.

"But the school year was approaching and I tried to pull myself together. I thought if I could concentrate on work I'd be okay. I was wrong – trying to concentrate on the upcoming school year was impossible. Nothing seemed to help. Then, one day, it was the day before school was to start... I just thought that since I'm too cowardly to kill myself quickly with a bullet or poison or jumping off a bridge, why not do it slowly, with alcohol. Dull the pain, drink myself into oblivion."

"That was the day you left Flint for life on the road? As a homeless guy?"

"I prefer the term urban camper. Yes, that was the day. I went home, packed a few things in my backpack and took off with the intention of drinking myself into the grave."

I try to imagine how that would feel, and how Geoff would feel now that he's no longer considered a person of suspicion. "Well, you know you don't need to run now. Do you think you still need to drink like that?"

"I see what you are saying. Once I talk to the cops it means I can stay in one place. But yes, I'm going to drink until I black out every day. In fact, speaking of that, I could use another martini."

I feel it, as I'm sitting there across from him. His nonchalance and glibness is getting to me. I have this incredible urge to grab him by the shoulders and shake him. I know I'm supposed to be impartial in all this; that's what makes investigative journalism successful. Impartially tell the story. Don't get personally involved with the subject matter. Stay balanced. But I can't. Finally, I blurt out, "You know, Geoff, you are not a super hero. In a way, you haven't changed a bit from the hockey kid who blew out his knee. You're afraid... and you do what you do when you're afraid – you hide behind substance abuse and self-pity. You say you are going to drink yourself into the grave, but that's not what this is really all about. You drink because you're afraid of adversity. And, you can't accept change. It's actually kind of pathetic."

His face contorts. Is it rage? Is it anguish? I continue. "You know, if you are blaming yourself about what happened to Martha and Jenny, that's just stupid. It doesn't matter who was driving that night... if you'd been driving and hit the moose you'd be dead, she'd be dead and Jenny would likely be dead too. If you'd swerved, well, rolling into the ditch would have had the same result. Call it fate. And, what about saving those children? Do you think that's fate? Or maybe it's all karma. You know, the yin and the yang of the universe. I've listened to your story. It seems there's a pattern of alternating good and bad things happening with you. Maybe the universe owed you, or owed those kids. Or, maybe all of this is divine intervention. I'm not religious, but they say 'God works in mysterious ways'. Maybe in this case, God worked in kind of a shitty way. Maybe you were set on this path to save those kids.

"Fate, karma, divine intervention. Take your pick. It doesn't really matter, because, in the end, your life is going to have peaks and valleys just like everyone else's. But Geoff, you can't let Martha down. Don't be that guy who banged up his knee and felt so sorry for himself he almost lost everything. Be the guy who accepted it, and went on to make a great life for himself. Don't let fate, karma or God decide what's left for Geoffrey Talbot. Be happy that you did some good by saving those kids, despite your self-destructive ways, then get back to being your best self. The guy who teaches and coaches and makes everyone around them want to succeed. Those are Samantha's words, but I'll

256

bet Martha would say the same damn thing."

I'm spent. It came out in a torrent. I look at Geoff. He's staring at me, shocked. I wonder if I've gone too far.

"Who the hell are you to talk to me like that!" he shouts at me, clearly enraged. I guess I shouldn't be surprised. His face then contorts from rage to anguish, and he lowers his head as his shoulders tremble with quiet sobbing. I've shaken him, badly. I'm not sure what to say next, so I say nothing. He gradually calms, then sits motionless for what seems like forever. He lifts his head and I see his features have relaxed into a look of astonishment.

Finally he speaks, "You know, Ms. Hope, I really wish I would've met you about five years ago. Although, maybe I wouldn't have been ready to hear it then. But, I know you're right. I've been a selfish, childish idiot. Martha would have told me much the same. And worse, I've been a coward. Just afraid to face my life. I don't know how just yet, but I'm going to put my life back together. I'm going to make Martha and Jenny proud of me." The tears come from both of us. Maybe aided by the melancholy effect of alcohol. But I see it in his eyes. He's sincere. Somehow, replaying his story has made him re-connect with the man that was Geoff Talbot.

It's been a long conversation. Much better than I could have ever hoped for. We are both emotionally drained, but, for the first time in a long time I feel like I've really connected with someone, outside of my writing. It reminds me of Darren. Maybe Geoff isn't the only one who's been running. We finish our meal. Geoff forgoes another martini as we each have a coffee and watch the sun slowly set. A heron stands at attention, scanning the shoreline for fish. Ducks swim in the pond, occasionally diving to forage. The cicadas start their long night song. It's time to head back to Jacksonville.

Epilogue

I submit my story just in time to meet the printing deadline, happy with the outcome.

But Jerome calls me the next day. "I'm sorry, Joanne, but I have some bad news. The financial crisis has finally caught up to me. I've taken some serious hits on some real estate deals. As a result, I can't afford my hobby any more... our beloved magazine is closing up shop."

I'm a bit surprised, but not overly. "Well, that really sucks. Are you going to be okay, Jerome?"

"Sure, I'll be fine. And you'll be fine too. I'll cover your expenses, like I promised. And check your bank account – I think you'll find your severance quite generous."

I'm verging on tears. Jerome has always had my back. "Thanks, Jerome. I'm really sorry how this is ending, but I know if there was any way to keep it going, you would have found it."

We say our goodbyes, promising to keep in touch, then I call Tony. Ever the asshole, Tony informs me that if the magazine wasn't folding he wouldn't have printed the story anyway. "Who wants to read about some drunk who just happens to be Johnny-on-the-spot for some heroics? Now, if he'd been the psychopath I'd hoped for, that would've been another matter."

"Hey, Tony... have a shitty life!" I slam the receiver down. But something has changed for me.

After meeting Geoff and hearing his story, I've come to realize that I can't waste my energy and time with the Tony's of this world.

These separate conversations with Jerome and Tony have put me in a reflective mood. For whatever reason I think about my mom.

When I was fifteen, Patsy finally met a man that changed both our lives. My stepfather Paul had been living in Ketchum for less than six months when he met Patsy at a local charity event. They struck up a conversation and found that they shared many of the same interests. Or, at least that's the story Patsy relies on. The story Paul relates is that Patsy applied for a receptionist/ bookkeeper job he'd posted for his booming construction company. However, regardless of how they first met, my mom did end up working for Paul, and, as is so often the case with my mom, what followed was a whirlwind romance. However, unlike her other post Chad romances, this one had a very happy ending for both of them, and by extension, me. Paul and Patsy married when I was seventeen. I remember her saying to me that she didn't have regrets about any part of her life, but did wish she had met Paul much sooner. Patsy thought she had won the lottery, but, in truth I think I was the winner. Paul quickly became the father I never had. He encouraged me to seek a scholarship, which I did get. He also augmented that scholarship. I can say with certainty that my odds of graduating from NYU would have been greatly diminished without Paul's generosity. I've always been proud of myself and what I've accomplished so far, but, upon reflection, I think I've been a bit myopic and prideful in thinking that everything I have and the person I've become is completely due to my own expended energy. The truth, I realize, is that it's the people you love and who love you back that really make the difference.

Since my episode with Geoff and my period of self-reflection, I've realized that I'm ever bit afraid of the future as Geoff is. Only, I don't have the trauma of losing those closest to me as rational for being so fragile. Lately I can't get Darren out of my mind, and the way I reacted to his proposal. I don't doubt I'd make the same decision if I had the ability to go back in time. I just wasn't ready for that commitment back then. But, it's been years. I realize I still love him. I realize I shouldn't be afraid of that anymore. I can't wait for fate, karma or divine intervention to bring us back together. I need to call him.

We have our usual back and forth banter. He makes me laugh. Then I tell update him about the story I'd just finished and my news: I'm unemployed.

Darren's reaction is music to my ears, "Well, why don't you come to St. Louis? I can put you up for a while; give you time to sort out what comes next. Who knows, maybe the Post-Dispatch could use a Pulitzer nominee, especially one that comes complete with an exclusive story."

I feign surprise, but I think Darren knows I'm ready. "Hey, that sounds great. I'm on my way. And

Darren... you know... all these years... "

      "Don't say it, Joanne. Just get yourself on a plane."

My time in rehab bought the various police departments time to retrace my steps prior to the 'incidents in question', to use their terminology, and to close their missing person cases. More importantly, they cleared me of any suspicion where the kids were concerned. They found Joey in St. Louis, who confirmed I'd been in the men's room when Flora decided to take a swim. They spoke with a few of my drinking companions in Victory Park in Nashville who confirmed my whereabouts when that poor little boy's mother OD'd and he almost roasted in the backseat of their car. And they spoke to Annette's neighbor, who confirmed he'd left anti-freeze under the kitchen sink, where Emmaline found it. I was officially off of all the hooks. I don't know who was more relieved, me or the cops.

Rehab also gave me time to think. A lot. I kept playing Joanne's words over and over in my head. Martha wouldn't want me to be afraid. Martha would want me to face life. But not just face it – she'd want me to live my life and be the best version of myself. And, to have a life with other people. It should not be an epiphany. I can't explain how it took a virtual stranger to point this out to me, other than to admit that I was afraid. I wasn't ready to face my life without Martha and Jenny. Drinking was my way of avoidance...or...maybe more accurately...a way to defer the inevitable.

And so, after six weeks in rehab in the sunny state of Florida, I returned to Flint. The house was no longer mine. Foreclosure – no surprise there; the mortgage far outstripped its market value. Like most of the homes in Flint, the financial crisis wreaked havoc on real estate prices. But that's okay. I was better off without that house anyway – too many memories.

I landed a job helping people dig their way out of debt as a debt consultant, and found a low-rent place to stay. I joined the local chapter of AA, and attended religiously every Wednesday night (and still do). That simple action helps me stay sober. My sponsor (a man in his mid-seventies named Charlie) visits my apartment on occasion now, helping me fight the demons that still creep up on me occasionally late at night.

I reconnected with Samantha and her husband Mark, and some of my old faculty friends. Some looked at me differently, and not always in a positive way. I don't blame them; it's a stigma that I brought upon myself. Nevertheless, for the most part, the community I left remained intact and most welcomed me back, and even supported me in ways that touched me deeply. A few of my former students would come by now and then to reminisce about their time on and off the ice with me.

I still had work to do mentally. I saw a therapist weekly (and still do), working on how I manage adversity and change. Every session with him, I'm reminded of Martha pulling me out of my depression when my NHL dreams were shattered and of Joanne Hope tracking me down and nudging me just enough to get me out of my self-destructive rut. I can never let events overwhelm me again. I know that now, but knowing it isn't enough. I have to live it, every single day.

Physically, I was told my liver showed signs of serious alcohol abuse. Had I continued on the path I was on for another year, or even months, it is likely I would have done irreparable damage. However, it turns out the liver is pretty resilient. Over time it will regenerate the cells that I recklessly killed during my dark days and nights. I still have abdominal pains now and then, but I've been reassured that if I continue to remain sober, this symptom should subside. The lasting physical side effect over which I have no control is that, due to my prolonged dance with the demon bottle, my odds of developing pancreatic or another form of cancer are significantly higher than your average middle aged male. I also have high blood pressure, which is being managed with dietary restrictions for now, but may require medication in the future. Overall, I feel I'm fortunate I've not have done more damage.

So, I feel I've made a lot of progress in re-integrating myself into the community I left behind all those years ago. For the most part, people have started to forget my past or, if acknowledged, it has been more about the tragic loss of Martha and Jenny and nothing is mentioned about my collapse. I think that for those that care about me, and even those who don't, it's simply easier that way.

I'd made my way to the rink many times to watch the Flint Flyers stumble their way through the regular season and one failed round of playoffs. They seemed to have a lot of talented kids, but I could see they weren't playing as a cohesive team. I couldn't help but pick apart their defensive schemes, their power plays, their penalty kills. Watching them play, it was hard to hide my disappointment and it was obvious others weren't happy with what they were seeing on the ice either.

It came as a surprise when Samantha took me aside this past spring before a Flyers' game and said, 'Geoff, I talked with the team head coach, Mike, on Friday. He told me that at the end of this school year he's resigning from Powers and he's going to take a job at another school. That means his teaching position will be open. And of course we can't afford to have a non-teaching head coach, so none of his assistant coaches would work as head coach. I have to clear it with the school board but I've spoken with most members and I don't think it'll be a problem... so... the teaching job's yours if you want it. And the head coach's. You can start in September. What do you say?"

We made quite the scene in the foyer. I picked her up, and spun her around. I kept saying 'Thank you, thank you!' We both laughed, and when I put her down, I noticed a few of the other teachers and even a few of my old students and players alumni were staring at us. Then Mark spontaneously started to clap. Then a few more joined in. Then a few more. Soon I was besieged with well-wishers. People clapping me on the back, saying, 'Welcome back, Geoff... we've missed you... great to see you back...". It was a wonderful feeling. I felt like I had a family again. Like I belonged.

True to her word, Samantha convinced the school board to hire me and I started back in September. I still think of Martha and my sweet Jenny every day, but, when I think of them now, I think of our happy times together. I think of the fragrance of Martha's hair when we lied in bed on Sunday mornings. I think of Jenny's laugh in the bubble bath. I don't think of my loss. At least, not as much.

When I do start to feel sorry for myself, I phone Joanne Hope, who has become somewhat of a confidant, and is always there for moral support. We shared something that very few people share. A moment of connection that made both of us step back and see our lives from a different perspective. That perspective slowing revealed a road to the future. A road that I started to realize I could navigate sober. Sometimes when I call Joanne, I get Darren, who, it turns out, despite his old email address, is not a big dick. We've become pretty good friends; they make me feel welcome in their lives.

It's funny how life has turned out. I often think of the kids I saved. How they are doing. If they remember what happened. Was it fate? Was it karma? Was it divine intervention? Take your pick. I don't know, and I probably never will, at least not in this life. But, one thing I can say for certain. Those kids weren't the only ones who were saved. I have them and Joanne, a now a whole supporting cast to thank for my new life, with all its ups and downs.

...The End.